Carol Marinelli recently filled in a form where she was asked for her job title and was thrilled, after all these years, to be able to put down her answer as 'writer'. Then it asked what Carol did for relaxation and, after chewing her pen for a moment, Carol put down the truth—'writing'. The third question asked, 'What are your hobbies?' Well, not wanting to look obsessed or, worse still, boring, she crossed the fingers on her free hand and answered 'swimming and tennis'. But, given that the chlorine in the pool does terrible things to her highlights, and the closest she's got to a tennis racket in the last couple of years is watching the Australian Open, I'm sure you can guess the real answer!

Recent books by Carol Marinelli:

Mills & Boon® Medical Romance™

NYC ANGELS: REDEEMING THE PLAYBOY**
SYDNEY HARBOUR HOSPITAL:
   AVA'S RE-AWAKENING*
HERS FOR ONE NIGHT ONLY?
CORT MASON—DR DELECTABLE
HER LITTLE SECRET
ST PIRAN'S: RESCUING PREGNANT CINDERELLA†
KNIGHT ON THE CHILDREN'S WARD

**NYC Angels
*Sydney Harbour Hospital
†St Piran's Hospital

Mills & Boon® Modern™ Romance

PLAYING THE DUTIFUL WIFE
BEHOLDEN TO THE THRONE~
BANISHED TO THE HAREM~
AN INDECENT PROPOSITION
A SHAMEFUL CONSEQUENCE
HEART OF THE DESERT
THE DEVIL WEARS KOLOVSKY

~Empire of the Sands

**These books are also available in eBook format
from www.millsandboon.co.uk**

Jasmine listened to the solemn voice of the newsreader telling viewers about a celebrity who was *resting* on the Peninsula after being found unconscious.

She got a glimpse of Jed walking by the stretcher as it was wheeled in. He was holding a sheet over the unfortunate patient's face. And then Jasmine watched as Mr Dean spoke, saying the patient was being transferred to ICU and there would be no further comment from the hospital.

It wasn't exactly riveting, so why did she rewind the feature?

Why did she freeze the screen?

Not in the hope of a glimpse at the celebrity.

And certainly not so she could listen again to Mr Dean.

It was Jed's face she paused on screen—and then she changed her mind.

She was over with anything remotely male, Jasmine reminded herself, and then turned as Simon, having finished his meal and now bored with the news, started bobbing in front of the television.

'Except you, little man.'

Dear Reader

I really enjoyed writing Penny and Jasmine's stories which make up my SECRETS ON THE EMERGENCY WING duet. Even though they are sisters they are very different and that is what made them so real to me. I loved that, even though they had the same parents and shared the same pasts, because of their unique personalities they looked at things differently.

Penny and Jasmine don't look alike; they don't even get on. No-one could even guess that they are sisters—they really are two different sides of the same coin. Yet, for all their differences, there are similarities and I had a lot of fun with a little secret of Penny's that you shan't find out till near the end of the second book.

I really would love to know which sister ends up being your favourite? Except, as my mother tells me, you're not allowed to have favourites…

You may yet be surprised ☺

Happy reading!

Carol

x

SECRETS ON THE EMERGENCY WING

Life and love—behind the doors of an Australian ER

Book 2 in Carol Marinelli's
SECRETS ON THE EMERGENCY WING duet

SECRETS OF A CAREER GIRL

is also available this month

The **SECRETS ON THE EMERGENCY WING**
duet is also available in eBook format
from www.millsandboon.co.uk

DR DARK AND FAR-TOO DELICIOUS

BY
CAROL MARINELLI

First published in Great Britain 2013
by Mills & Boon, an imprint of Harlequin (UK) Limited.
Harlequin (UK) Limited, Eton House, 18-24 Paradise Road,
Richmond, Surrey TW9 1SR

© Carol Marinelli 2013

ISBN: 978 0 263 23367 4

CHAPTER ONE

JUST CONCENTRATE ON WORK.

Jed said it over and over as he ran along the damp beach.

He ran daily, or tried to, depending on work commitments, but as much as he could Jed factored running into his day—it served as both his exercise and his relaxation, helped him to focus and to clear his head.

Just concentrate on work, he repeated, because after the last two hellish years he really did need to do just that.

Jed looked along the bay. The morning was a hazy one and he couldn't make out the Melbourne skyline in the distance. Not for the first time he questioned whether he had been right to take the position at the Peninsula Hospital or if he should have gone for a more prestigious city one.

Jed loved nothing more than a big city hospital—he had worked and trained at a large teaching hospital in Sydney and had assumed, when he had applied for jobs in Melbourne, that the city was where he would end up, yet the interview at Peninsula Hospital that he had thought would be a more a cursory one had seen him change his mind.

It wasn't a teaching hospital but it was certainly a busy one—it served as a major trauma centre and had an NICU and ICU and Jed had liked the atmosphere at Peninsula, as well as the proximity to the beach. Perhaps the deciding factor, though, had been that he had also been told, confidentially, that one of the consultants was retiring and a position would be opening up in the not-too-distant future. His career had been building up to an emergency consultant position and, his disaster of a personal life aside, it was where he was ready to be. When Jed had handed in his notice six months ago an offer had been made and he'd been asked to reconsider leaving, but Jed had known then that he had to get away, that he had to start again.

But with new rules in place this time.

Jed missed not just Sydney and the hospital he had trained and worked at but his family and friends—it had been the first birthday of Luke, his newest nephew, yesterday, another thing he hadn't been able to get to, another family gathering he had missed, when before, even if he hadn't been able to get there on the day, he'd have dropped by over the weekend.

A phone call to a one-year-old wasn't exactly the same.

But the decision to move well away had surely been the right one.

Still he questioned it, still he wondered if he had over-reacted and should have just stayed in Sydney and hoped it would work out, assumed it was all sorted.

What a mess.

Jed stopped for a moment and dragged in a few breaths.

Over and over he wondered if he could have handled

things differently, if there was something he could have said to have changed things, or something he had done that had been misconstrued—and yet still he could not come up with an answer.

It was incredibly warm for six a.m. but it wasn't a pleasant heat—it was muggy and close and needed a good storm to clear it but, according to the weather reports, the cool change wasn't coming through till tonight.

'Morning.' He looked up and nodded to an old guy walking his dog. They shared a brief conversation about the weather and then Jed took a long drink of water before turning around to head for home and get ready for work.

He should never have got involved with Samantha in the first place.

Still, he could hardly have seen that coming, couldn't have predicted the train wreck that had been about to take place, but then he corrected himself.

He should never have got involved with someone from work.

Jed picked up the pace again, his head finally clearing. He knew what he needed to focus on.

Just concentrate on work.

CHAPTER TWO

'JASMINE?' IT WASN'T the friendliest of greetings, and Jasmine jumped as the sound of Penny's voice stopped her in her tracks.

'What are you doing here?' her sister demanded.

'I'm here for an interview.' Jasmine stated what should be the obvious. 'I've just been for a security check.'

They were standing in the hospital admin corridor. Jasmine was holding a pile of forms and, despite her best efforts to appear smart and efficient for the interview, was looking just a little hot and bothered—and all the more so for seeing Penny.

Summer had decided to give Melbourne one last sticky, humid day before it gave way to autumn and Jasmine's long dark curls had, despite an awful lot of hair serum and an awful lot of effort, frizzed during the walk from the car park to the accident and emergency department. It had continued its curly journey through her initial interview with Lisa, the nurse unit manager.

Now, as Penny ran a brief but, oh, so critical eye over her, Jasmine was acutely aware that the grey suit she reserved for interviews was, despite hundreds of sit-ups and exercising to a DVD, just a touch too tight.

Penny, of course, looked immaculate.

Her naturally straight, naturally blonde hair was tied back in an elegant chignon—she was wearing smart dark trousers and heeled shoes that accentuated her lean body. Her white blouse, despite it being afternoon, despite the fact she was a registrar in a busy accident and emergency department, was still impossibly crisp and clean.

No one could have guessed that they were sisters.

'An interview for what, exactly?' Penny's eyes narrowed.

'A nursing position,' Jasmine answered carefully. 'A clinical nurse specialist. I've just been to fill out the forms for a security check.' Jasmine was well aware her answer was vague and that she was evading the issue but of course it didn't work—Penny was as direct as ever in her response.

'Where?' Penny asked. 'Where exactly have you applied to work?'

'Accident and Emergency,' Jasmine answered, doing her best to keep her voice even. 'Given that it's my speciality.'

'Oh, no.' Penny shook her head. 'No way.' Penny made no effort to keep her voice even, and she didn't mince her words either. 'I'm not having it, Jasmine, not for a single moment. You are *not* working in my department.'

'Where do you expect me to work, then, Penny?' She had known all along that this would be Penny's reaction—it was the very reason she had put off telling her sister about the application, the very reason she hadn't mentioned the interview when they had met up at Mum's last Sunday for a celebratory dinner to toast

Penny's *latest* career victory. 'I'm an emergency nurse, that's what I do.'

'Well, go and do it somewhere else. Go and work at the hospital you trained in, because there is no way on earth that I am working alongside my sister.'

'I can't commute to the city,' Jasmine said. 'Do you really expect me to drag Simon for an hour each way just so that I don't embarrass my big sister?' It was ridiculous to suggest and what was even more ridiculous was that Jasmine had actually considered it, well aware how prickly Penny could be.

Jasmine had looked into it, but with a one-year-old to consider, unless she moved nearer to the city, it would prove impossible and also, in truth, she was just too embarrassed to go back to her old workplace.

'You know people there,' Penny insisted.

'Exactly.'

'Jasmine, if the reason you're not going back there is because of Lloyd…'

'Leave it, Penny.' Jasmine closed her eyes for a second. She didn't want to go back to where everyone knew her past, where her life had been the centre stage show for rather too long. 'It has nothing to do with Lloyd. I just want to be closer to home.'

She did—with her marriage completely over and her soon-to-be ex-husband having nothing to do with either her or her son and her maternity leave well and truly up, Jasmine had made the decision to move back to the beachside suburb to be close to the family home and the smart townhouse where her sister lived and to start over again, but with family nearby.

She wanted to be closer to her mum, to her sister and,

yes, she wanted some support, but clearly she wasn't going to get any from Penny.

It was career first, last and always for Penny, but then again it was the same with their mum. A real estate agent, though now semi-retired, Louise Masters had made a name for herself in their bayside village for being tough and no-nonsense. It was the rather more dreamy Jasmine who did stupid things like take risks with her heart and actually switch off from work on her days off—not that she didn't love her work, it just wasn't all that she was.

'We'll talk about this later.' Penny's blue eyes flashed angrily—it was the only feature that they shared. 'And don't you dare go using my name to get the job.'

'As if I'd do that,' Jasmine said. 'Anyway, we don't even share the same surname, *Miss* Masters.'

Penny was now officially a Miss—the title given to females once they gained their fellowship. It caused some confusion at times, but Penny had worked extremely hard to be a Miss rather than a Doctor—and she wasn't about to have anyone drag on her coat-tails as she continued to ride high.

'I mean it,' Penny flared. 'You are not to even let on that you know me. I'm really not happy about this, Jasmine.'

'Hey, Penny.' Her sister turned, and so too did Jasmine, to the sound of a deep, low voice. Had Jasmine not been so numb right now, so immune and resistant to all things male, she might have more properly noticed just how good looking this man was. He was very tall and though his dark brown hair was cut fairly short it was just a bit rumpled, as was his suit.

Yes, a couple of years ago she might have taken note, but not now.

She just wanted him gone so that she could get back to the rather important conversation she had been having with Penny.

'It's getting busy down there apparently,' he said to Penny. 'They just called and asked me to come back from lunch.'

'I know,' came Penny's clipped response. 'I've just been paged. I was supposed to be speaking with Legal.'

Perhaps he picked up on the tension because he looked from Penny to Jasmine and she noticed then that his eyes were green and that his jaw needed shaving and, yes, despite being completely not interested, some long-dormant cells demanded that she at least deign to acknowledge just how attractive he was, especially when his deep voice spoke on. 'Sorry, am I disturbing something?'

'Not at all.' Penny's response was rapid. 'This nurse was just asking for directions to get back to Emergency—she's got an interview there.'

'You can hardly miss the place.' He gave a wry smile and nodded to a huge red arrow above them. 'Follow us.'

'Mrs Phillips?' Jasmine turned as she heard her name and saw it was the receptionist from Security, where she had just come from. 'You left your driving licence.'

'Thank you.' Jasmine opened her mouth to say that she was soon to be a Ms, but it seemed churlish to correct it as technically she was still a Mrs—it was there on her driving licence after all. Still, in a few weeks' time she'd be a Ms and she'd tell everyone the same.

Jasmine couldn't wait for the glorious day.

For now, though, she followed Penny and her colleague towards Emergency.

'I didn't mean to literally follow,' Jed said, and he waited a second for her to catch up. Jasmine fell into reluctant step alongside them. 'I'm Jed…Jed Devlin—I'm a registrar in the madhouse, as is Penny.'

'Jasmine.' She duly answered. 'Jasmine Phillips.'

'So?' he asked as Penny clipped noisily alongside them. She could hear the anger in her sister's footsteps, could feel the tension that was ever present whenever the two of them were together. 'When do you start?'

'I haven't got the job yet,' Jasmine said.

'Sounds promising, though, if you've been sent up to Security.'

'They have to do a security check on everyone,' Penny said abruptly.

They all walked on in silence for a few moments.

'Here we are,' Jed said. 'See that big red sign that says "Accident and Emergency"?'

'How could I miss it?' She gave a brief smile at his teasing as they headed through the swing doors and stepped into Emergency. 'Thanks.'

'No problem.'

'Good luck,' Jed said.

Of course Penny didn't offer her best wishes. Instead, she marched off on her high heels and for a second Jasmine stood there and blew out a breath, wondering if she was mad to be doing this.

It clearly wasn't going to work.

And then she realised that Jed was still standing there.

'Do I know you?' He frowned.

'I don't think so,' Jasmine said, while reluctantly admitting to herself that they had definitely never met—his was a face she certainly wouldn't forget.

'Have you worked in Sydney?'

Jasmine shook her head.

'Where did you work before?'

She started to go red. She hated talking about her time there—she'd loved it so much and it had all ended so terribly, but she could hardly tell him that. 'Melbourne Central. I trained there and worked in Emergency there till I had my son.'

'Nice hospital,' Jed said. 'I had an interview there when I first moved to the area, but no.' He shook his head. 'That's not it. You just look familiar…'

He surely hadn't picked up that she and Penny were sisters? No one ever had. She and Penny were complete opposites, not just in looks but also in personality. Penny was completely focussed and determined, whereas Jasmine was rather more impulsive, at least she had been once. She was also, as her mother had frequently pointed out throughout her childhood whenever Jasmine had burst into tears, too sensitive.

'There you are!' Jasmine turned as Lisa came over and Jed made his excuses and wandered off.

'Sorry,' Jasmine said to Lisa. 'They took ages to find all the forms I needed.'

'That's Admin for you,' Lisa said. 'Right, I'll walk you through the department and give you a feel for the place. It just got busy.'

It certainly had.

It had been almost empty when Jasmine had first arrived for her interview and the walk to Lisa's office had shown a calm, even quiet department, compared to the busy city one Jasmine was more used to. Now, though, the cubicles were all full and she could see staff rushing and hear the emergency bell trilling from Resus. Not for the first time, Jasmine wondered if she was up to the demands of going back to work in a busy emergency department.

The last two years had left her so raw and confused that all she really wanted to do was to curl up and sleep before she tackled the process of healing and resuming work, but her ex didn't want to see their son, let alone pay child support, and there was no point going through appropriate channels—she couldn't wait the time it would take to squeeze blood from a stone, but more than that Jasmine wanted to support her son herself, which meant that she needed a job.

However much it inconvenienced Penny and however daunted she was at the prospect.

'We do our best with the roster. I always try to accommodate specific requests, but as far as regular shifts go I can't make allowances for anyone,' Lisa explained—she knew about Simon and had told Jasmine that there were a couple of other single mums working there who, she was sure, would be a huge support. 'And I've rung the crèche and said that you'll be coming over to have a look around, but you know that they close at six and that on a late shift you don't generally get out till well after nine?'

Jasmine nodded. 'My mum's said that she'll help out for a little while.' Jasmine stated this far more generously than her mother had. 'At least until I sort out a babysitter.'

'What about night shifts?' Lisa checked. 'Everyone has to do them—it's only fair.'

'I know.'

'That way,' Lisa explained, 'with everyone taking turns, generally it only comes around once every three months or so.'

'That sounds fine,' Jasmine said confidently while inwardly gauging her mother's reaction.

It was a good interview, though. Really, Jasmine was confident that she'd got the job and, as she left, Lisa practically confirmed it. 'You'll be hearing from us soon.' She gave a wry smile as Jasmine shook her hand. 'Very soon. I wish you didn't have to do orientation before you start—I've just had two of my team ring in sick for the rest of the week.'

Walking towards the exit, Jasmine saw how busy yet efficient everyone looked and despite her confident words about her experience to Lisa, inside she was a squirming mess! Even though she'd worked right up to the end of her pregnancy she hadn't nursed in more than a year and, again, she considered going back to her old department. At least she'd maybe know a few people.

At least she'd know where things were kept. Yet there would still be the nudges and whispers that she'd been so relieved to leave behind and, yes, she should just walk in with her head held high and face the ugly rumours and gossip, except going back to work after all she had been through was already hard enough.

'Jasmine?' She turned as someone called her name and forced back on her smile when she saw that it was Jed. He was at the viewfinder looking at an X-ray. 'How did you get on?'

'Good,' Jasmine answered. 'Well, at least I think I did.'

'Well done.'

'I'm just going to check out the crèche.'

'Good luck again, then,' Jed said, 'because from what I've heard you'll need it to get a place there.'

'Oh, and, Jasmine,' he called as she walked off, 'I do know you.'

'You don't.' Jasmine laughed.

'But I know that I do,' he said. 'I never forget a face. I'll work it out.'

She rather hoped that he wouldn't.

CHAPTER THREE

'HOW DID YOU GO?' her mum asked as she let her in.

'Well,' Jasmine said. 'Sorry that it took so long.'

'That's okay. Simon's asleep.' Jasmine followed her mum through to the kitchen and Louise went to put the kettle on. 'So when do you start?'

'I don't even know if I've got the job.'

'Please,' her mum said over her shoulder. 'Everywhere's screaming for nurses, you hear it on the news all the time.'

It was a backhanded compliment—her mother was very good at them. Jasmine felt the sting of tears behind her eyes—Louise had never really approved of Jasmine going into nursing. Her mother had told her that if she worked a bit harder at school she could get the grades and study medicine, just like Penny. And though she never came right out and said it, it was clear that in both her mother's and sister's eyes Penny had a career whereas Jasmine had a job—and one that could be done by anyone—as if all that Jasmine had to do was put on her uniform and show up.

'It's a clinical nurse specialist role that I've applied for, Mum,' Jasmine said. 'There were quite a few applicants.' But her mum made no comment and not for the first time Jasmine questioned her decision to move close to home. Her mum just wasn't mumsy—she was successful in everything she did. She was funny, smart and career-minded, and she simply expected her daughters to be the same—after all, she'd juggled her career and had independently raised Jasmine and Penny when their father had walked out.

Jasmine wanted nothing more than to be independent and do the same; she just wanted a pause, a bit of a helping hand as she got through this bit—which in her own way her mother had given. After four weeks of living at home Louise had had a very nice little rental house come onto her books—it was right on the beach and the rent was incredibly low and Jasmine had jumped at it. It was in other areas that Jasmine was struggling, and nursing with all its shift work wasn't an easy career to juggle without support.

'I'm going to have to do nights.' Jasmine watched her mother's shoulders stiffen as she filled two mugs. 'A fortnight every three months.'

'I didn't raise two children just so that I could raise yours,' Louise warned. 'I'll help you as much as I can for a couple of months, but I take a lot of clients through houses in the evenings.' She was as direct as ever. 'And I've got my cruise booked for May.'

'I know,' Jasmine said. 'I'm going to start looking for a regular babysitter as soon as I get the offer.'

'And you need to give me your off duty at least a month in an advance.'

'I will.'

Jasmine took the tea from her mum. If she wanted a hug she wasn't going to get one; if she wanted a little pick me up she was in the wrong house.

'Have you thought about looking for a job that's a bit more child friendly?' Louise suggested. 'You mentioned there was one in Magnetic…' She gave an impatient shrug when she couldn't remember the terminology.

'No. I said there was a position in MRI and that even though the hours were fantastic it wasn't what I wanted to do. I like Emergency, Mum. You wouldn't suggest Penny going for a role she had no interest in.'

'Penny doesn't have a one-year-old to think of,' Louise said, and then they sat quietly for a moment.

'You need to get your hair done,' her mum said. 'You need to smarten up a bit if you're going back to work.' And that was her mum's grudging way of accepting that, yes, this was what Jasmime was going to do. 'And you need to lose some weight.'

And because it was either that or start crying, Jasmine chose to laugh.

'What's so funny?'

'You are,' Jasmine said. 'I thought tea came with sympathy.'

'Not in this house.' Her mum smiled. 'Why don't you go home?'

'Simon's asleep.'

'I'll have him for you tonight.'

And sometimes, and always when Jasmine was least expecting it, her mum could be terribly nice. 'My evening appointment cancelled. I'm sure you could use a night to yourself.'

'I'd love that.' Jasmine hadn't had a night to herself since Simon had been born. In the weeks when she'd first come home and had stayed with her mum, the only advantage she had taken had been a long walk on the beach each morning before Simon woke up. 'Thanks, Mum.'

'No problem. I guess I'd better get familiar with his routines.'

'Can I go in and see him?'

'And wake him up probably.'

She didn't wake him up. Simon was lying on his front with his bottom in the air and his thumb in his mouth, and just the sight of him made everything worth it. He was in her old cot in her old bedroom and was absolutely the love of her life. She just didn't understand how Lloyd could want nothing to do with him.

'Do you think he's missing out?' Jasmine asked her mum. 'Not having a dad?'

'Better no dad than a useless one,' Louise said, then gave a shrug. 'I don't know the answer to that, Jasmine. I used to feel the same about you.' She gave her daughter a smile. 'Our taste in men must be hereditary. No wonder Penny's sworn off them.'

'Did she ever tell you what happened?' Jasmine asked, because one minute Penny had been engaged, the next the whole thing had been called off and she didn't want to talk about it.

'She just said they'd been having a few problems and decided that it was better to get out now than later.'

Before there were children to complicate things, Jasmine thought, but didn't say anything. It was her mum who spoke.

'I know it's tough at the moment but I'm sure it will get easier.'

'And if it doesn't?'

'Then you'd better get used to tough.' Louise shrugged. 'Have you told Penny you're applying for a job at Peninsula?'

'I saw her at my interview.'

'And?' Louise grimaced. They both knew only too well how Penny would react to the news.

'She doesn't want me there—especially not in Accident and Emergency,' Jasmine admitted. 'She wasn't best pleased.'

'Well, it's her domain,' Louise said. 'You know how territorial she is. She used to put thread up on her bedroom door so she'd know if anyone had been in there while she was out. She'll come round.'

And even though she smiled at the memory, Jasmine was worried that Penny wouldn't be coming round to the idea of her little sister working in her hospital any time soon.

Jasmine was proven right a few hours later when, back at her own small house, adding another coat of paint in an attempt to transform the lounge from dull olive green to cool crisp white, there was a loud rap at the door.

'Can you knock more quietly?' Jasmine asked as she opened it. 'If Simon was here—'

'We need to talk,' Penny said, and she brushed in and straight through to the lounge.

If Louise hadn't exactly been brimming with understanding, then Penny was a desert.

Her blouse was still crisp and white, her hair still perfect and her eyes were just as angry as they had been when she had first laid them on Jasmine in the hospital corridor earlier on that day. 'You said nothing about this when I saw you last week,' Penny said accusingly. 'Not a single word!'

'I didn't exactly get a chance.'

'Meaning?'

She heard the confrontation in her sister's voice, could

almost see Pandora's box on the floor between them. She was tempted just to open it, to have this out once and for all, to say how annoyed she still felt that Penny hadn't been able to make it for Simon's first birthday a couple of months earlier. In fact, she hadn't even sent a card. Yet there had been no question that Jasmine herself would be there to join in celebrating her sister's success.

Or rather celebrating her sister's *latest* success.

But bitterness wasn't going to help things here.

'That dinner was to celebrate you getting your fellowship,' Jasmine said calmly. 'I knew you'd be upset if I told you that I had an interview coming up, and I didn't want to spoil your night.'

'You should have discussed it with me before you even applied!' Penny said. 'It's my department.'

'Hopefully it will be mine soon, too,' Jasmine attempted, but her words fell on deaf ears.

'Do you know how hard it is for me?' Penny said. 'All that nonsense about equal rights... I have to be twice as good as them, twice as tough as any of them—there's a consultancy position coming up and I have no intention of letting it slip by.'

'How could my working there possibly affect that?' Jasmine asked reasonably.

'Because I'm not supposed to have a personal life,' was Penny's swift retort. 'You just don't get it, Jasmine. I've worked hard to get where I am. The senior consultant, Mr Dean, he's old school—he made a joke the other week about how you train them up and the next thing you know they're pregnant and wanting part-time hours.' She looked at her sister. 'Yes, I could complain and make waves, but how is that going to help things? Jed is going after the same position. He's a great doctor but he's only been in the department six months and I am not going to lose it to him.' She shook her head in frustration.

'I'm not asking you to understand, you just have to believe that it is hard to get ahead sometimes, and the last thing I need right now is my personal life invading the department.'

'I'm your sister—'

'So are you going to be able to stay quiet when the nurses call me a hard witch?' Penny challenged. 'And when you are supposed to finish at four but can't get off, are you going to expect me to drop everything and run to the crèche and get Simon?'

'Of course not.'

'And when I hear the other nurses moaning that you hardly ever do a late shift and are complaining about having to do nights, am I supposed to leap to your defence and explain that you're a single mum?'

'I can keep my work and personal life separate.'

'Really!'

It was just one word, a single word, and the rise of Penny's perfect eyebrows had tears spring to Jasmine's eyes. 'That was below the belt.'

'The fact that you can't keep your work and personal life separate is the very reason you can't go back to Melbourne Central.'

'It's about the travel,' Jasmine insisted. 'And you're wrong, I can keep things separate.'

'Not if we're in the same department.'

'I can if they don't know that we're sisters,' Jasmine said, and she watched Penny's jaw tighten, realised then that this was where the conversation had been leading. Penny was always one step ahead in everything, and

Penny had made very sure that it was Jasmine who suggested it.

'It might be better.' Penny made it sound as if she was conceding.

'Fine.'

'Can you keep to it?'

'Sure,' Jasmine said.

'I mean it.'

'I know you do, Penny.'

'I've got to get back to work. I'm on call tonight.' And her sister, now that she had what she came for, stood up to leave. Jasmine held in tears that threatened, even managed a smile as her sister stalked out of the door.

But it hurt.

It really hurt.

CHAPTER FOUR

IT WAS HER favourite place in the world.

But even a long stretch of sand, the sun going down over the water and a storm rolling in from the distance wasn't enough to take the harsh sting out of Penny's words.

Jasmine hated arguments, loathed them and did her very best to avoid them.

She could still remember all too well hearing the raised voices of her parents seeping up the stairs and through the bedroom floor as she had lain on her bed with her hands over her ears.

But there had been no avoiding this one—Jasmine had known when she'd applied for the role that there would be a confrontation. Still, she couldn't just bow to Penny's wishes just because it made things awkward for her.

She needed a job and, no matter what her mother and sister thought of her chosen career, nursing was what she was good at—and Emergency was her speciality.

Jasmine wasn't going to hide just because it suited Penny.

It had been cruel of Penny to bring up her relationship with Lloyd, cruel to suggest that she wasn't going back to Melbourne Central just because of what had happened.

It was also, Jasmine conceded, true.

Finding out that she was pregnant had been a big enough shock—but she'd had no idea what was to come.

That the dashing paramedic who'd been so delighted with the news of her pregnancy, who'd insisted they marry and then whisked her off on a three-month honeymoon around Australia, was in fact being investigated for patient theft.

She'd been lied to from the start and deceived till the end and nothing, it seemed, could take away her shame. And, yes, the whispers and sideways looks she had received from her colleagues at Melbourne Central as she'd worked those last weeks of her pregnancy with her marriage falling apart had been awful. The last thing she needed was Penny rubbing it in.

'I knew I recognised you from somewhere.' She looked over to the sound of a vaguely familiar voice.

'Oh!' Jasmine was startled as she realised who it was. 'Hi, Jed.' He was out of breath from running and—she definitely noticed this time—was very, very good looking.

He was wearing grey shorts and a grey T-shirt and he was toned, a fact she couldn't fail to notice when he lifted his T-shirt to wipe his face, revealing a very flat, tanned stomach. Jasmine felt herself blush as for the first time in the longest time she was shockingly drawn to rugged maleness.

But, then, how could you not be? Jasmine reasoned. Any woman hauled out of a daydream would blink a few times when confronted with him. Any woman would be a bit miffed that they hadn't bothered sorting their hair and that they were wearing very old denim shorts and a T-shirt splashed with paint.

'You walk here?' Jed checked, because now he remembered her. Dark curls bobbing, she would walk—sometimes slowly, sometimes briskly and, he had noticed she never looked up, never acknowledged anyone—she always seemed completely lost in her own world. 'I see you some mornings,' Jed said, and then seemed to think about it. 'Though not for a while.'

'I live just over there.' Jasmine pointed to her small weatherboard house. 'I walk here every chance I get—though I haven't had too many chances of late.'

'We're almost neighbours.' Jed smiled. 'I'm in the one on the end.' He nodded towards the brand-new group of town houses a short distance away that had been built a couple of years ago. Her mother had been the agent in a couple of recent sales there and Jasmine wondered if one of them might have been to him.

And just to remind her that he hadn't specifically noticed her, he nodded to another jogger who went past, and as they walked along a little way, he said hi to an elderly couple walking their dog. He clearly knew the locals.

'Taking a break from painting?' He grinned.

'How did you guess?' Jasmine sighed. 'I don't know who's madder—whoever painted the wall green, or me for thinking a couple of layers of white would fix it. I'm on my third coat.' She looked over at him and then stated the obvious. 'So you run?'

'Too much,' Jed groaned. 'It's addictive.'

'Not for me,' Jasmine admitted. 'I tried, but I don't really know where to start.'

'You just walk,' Jed said, 'and then you break into a run and then walk again—you build up your endurance. It doesn't take long.' He smiled. 'See? I'm addicted.'

'No, I get it.' Jasmine grinned back. 'I just don't do it.'

'So, how did you go with the crèche?' He walked along beside her and Jasmine realised he was probably just catching his breath, probably pacing himself rather than actually stopping for her. Still, it was nice to have a chat.

'They were really accommodating, though I think Lisa might have had something to do with that.'

'How old is your child?'

'Fourteen months,' Jasmine said. 'His name's Simon.'

'And is this your first job since he was born?' He actually did seem to want to talk her. Jasmine had expected that he'd soon jog off, but instead he walked along beside her, his breathing gradually slowing down. It was nice to have adult company, nice to walk along the beach and talk.

'It is,' Jasmine said. 'And I'm pretty nervous.'

'You worked at Melbourne Central, though,' he pointed out. 'That's one hell of a busy place. It was certainly buzzing when I went for my interview there.'

'Didn't you like it?'

'I did,' Jed said, 'but I was surprised how much I liked Peninsula Hospital. I was sort of weighing up between the two and this…' he looked out to the bay, '…was a huge draw card. The beach is practically next to the hospital and you can even see it from the canteen.'

'I'm the same,' Jasmine said, because as much as she loved being in the city she was a beach girl through and through.

'You'll be fine,' Jed said. 'It will take you ten minutes to get back into the swing of things.'

'I think it might take rather more than that.' Jasmine laughed. 'Having a baby scrambles your brains a bit.

Still, it will be nice to be working again. I've just got to work out all the shifts and things.'

'What does your husband do?' Jed took a swig from his water bottle. 'Can he help?'

'We're separated,' Jasmine replied.

'Oh. I'm sorry to hear that.'

'It's fine,' Jasmine said. She was getting used to saying it and now, just as she was, it would be changing again because she'd be divorced.

It was suddenly awkward; the conversation that had flowed so easily seemed to have come to a screeching halt. 'Storm's getting close.' Jed nodded out to the distance.

Given they were now reduced to talking about the weather, Jasmine gave a tight smile. 'I'd better go in and watch my paint dry.'

'Sure,' Jed said, and gave her a smile before he jogged off.

And as she turned and headed up to her flat she wanted to turn, wanted to call out to his rapidly departing back, *'It's okay, you don't have to run—just because I don't have a partner doesn't mean that I'm looking for another one.'*

God, talk about put the wind up him.

Still, she didn't dwell on it.

After all there were plenty of other things on her mind without having to worry about Jed Devlin.

CHAPTER FIVE

THERE WAS, JASMINE decided, one huge advantage to being related to two fabulously strong, independent women.

It sort of forced you to be fabulously strong and independent yourself, even when you didn't particularly feel it.

The hospital squeezed her in for that month's orientation day and after eight hours of fire drills, uniform fittings, occupational health and safety lectures and having her picture taken for her lanyard, she was officially on the accident and emergency roster. Lisa had, as promised, rung the crèche and told them Simon was a priority, due to the shortage of regular staff in Emergency.

So, just over a week later at seven o'clock on a Wednesday morning, two kilograms lighter thanks to a new diet, and with her hair freshly cut, Jasmine dropped her son off for his first day of crèche.

'Are you sure he's yours?' Shona, the childcare worker grinned as Jasmine handed him over. It was a reaction she got whenever anyone saw her son, even the midwives had teased her in the maternity ward. Simon was so blond and long and skinny that Jasmine felt as if she'd borrowed someone else's baby at times.

Until he started to cry, until he held out his arms to Jasmine the moment that he realised he was being left.

Yep, Jasmine thought, giving him a final cuddle, he might look exactly like Penny but, unlike his aunt, he was as soft as butter—just like his mum.

'Just go,' Shona said when she saw that Simon's mum looked as if she was about to start crying too. 'You're five minutes away and we'll call if you're needed, but he really will be fine.'

And so at seven-twenty, a bit red-nosed and glassy-eyed, Jasmine stood by the board and waited for handover to start.

She never even got to hear it.

'I've decided to pair you with Vanessa,' Lisa told her. 'For the next month you'll do the same shifts, and, as far as we can manage, you'll work alongside her. I've put the two of you in Resus this morning so don't worry about handover. It's empty for now so I'll get Vanessa to show you around properly while it's quiet—it won't stay that way for long.'

'Sure,' Jasmine said, in many ways happy to be thrown straight in at the deep end, rather than spending time worrying about it. And Lisa didn't have much choice. There wasn't much time for handholding—experienced staff were thin on the ground this morning, and even though she hadn't nursed in a year, her qualifications and experience were impressive and Lisa needed her other experienced nurses out in the cubicles to guide the agency staff they had been sent to help with the patient ratio shortfalls this morning.

Vanessa was lovely.

She had been working at the hospital for three years, she told Jasmine, and while it was empty, she gave her a more thorough tour of the resuscitation area as they checked the oxygen and suction and that everything was stocked. She also gave her a little bit of gossip along the way.

'There's Mr Dean.' Vanessa pulled a little face. 'He likes things done his way and it takes a little while to work that out, but once you do he's fine,' she explained as they checked and double-checked the equipment. 'Rex and Helena are the other consultants.' Jasmine found she was holding her breath more than a little as Vanessa worked through the list of consultants and registrars and a few nurses and gave titbits of gossip here and there.

'Penny Masters, Senior Reg.' Vanessa rolled her eyes. 'Eats lemons for breakfast, so don't take anything personally. She snaps and snarls at everyone and jumps in uninvited,' Vanessa said, 'but you have to hand it to her, she does get the job done. And then there's Jed.' Jasmine realised that she was still holding her breath, waiting to hear about him.

'He's great to work with too, a bit brusque, keeps himself to himself.' Funny, Jasmine thought, he hadn't seemed anything other than friendly when she had met him, but, still, she didn't dwell on it. They soon had their first patients coming through and were alerted to expect a patient who had fallen from scaffolding. He had arm fractures but, given the height from which he had fallen, there was the potential for some serious internal injuries, despite the patient being fully conscious. Resus was prepared and Jasmine felt her shoulders tense as Penny walked in, their eyes meeting for just a brief second as Penny tied on a large plastic apron and put on protective glasses and gloves.

'This is Jasmine,' Vanessa happily introduced her. 'The new clinical nurse specialist.'

'What do we know about the patient?' was Penny's tart response.

Which set the tone.

The patient was whizzed in. He was young, in pain and called Cory, and Penny shouted orders as he was moved carefully over onto the trolley on the spinal board. He was covered in plaster dust. It was in his hair, on his clothes and in his eyes, and it blew everywhere as they tried to cut his clothes off. Despite Cory's arms being splinted, he started to thrash about on the trolley

'Just stay nice and still, Cory.' Jasmine reassured the patient as Penny thoroughly examined him—listening to his chest and palpating his abdomen, demanding his observations even before he was fully attached to the equipment and then ordering some strong analgesia for him.

'My eyes…' Cory begged, even when the pain medication started to hit, and Penny checked them again.

'Can you lavage his eyes?' Penny said, and Jasmine warmed a litre of saline to a tepid temperature and gently washed them out as Penny spoke to the young man.

'Right,' Penny said to her young patient. 'We're going to get some X-rays and CTs, but so far it would seem you've been very lucky.'

'Lucky?' Cory checked.

'She means compared to how it might have been,' Jasmine said as she continued to lavage his eyes. 'You fell from quite a height and, judging by the fact you've got two broken wrists, well, it looks like as if you managed to turn and put out your hands to save yourself,' Jasmine explained. 'Which probably doesn't feel very lucky right now.

'How does that eye feel?' She wiped his right eye with gauze and Cory blinked a few times.

'Better.'

'How's the pain now?'

'A bit better.'

'Need any help?' Jasmine looked up at the sound of Jed's voice. He smelt of morning, all fresh and brisk and ready to help, but Penny shook her head.

'I've got this.' She glanced over to another patient being wheeled in. 'He might need your help, though.'

She'd forgotten this about Emergency—you didn't get a ten-minute break to catch your breath and tidy up, and more often than not it was straight into the next one. As Vanessa, along with Penny, dealt with X-rays and getting Cory ready for CT, Jasmine found herself working alone with Jed on his patient, with Lisa popping in and out.

'It's her first day!' Lisa warned Jed as she opened some equipment while Jasmine connected the patient to the monitors as the paramedics gave the handover.

'No problem,' Jed said, introducing himself to the elderly man and listening to his chest as Jasmine attached him to monitors and ran off a twelve-lead ECG. The man was in acute LVF, meaning his heart was beating ineffectively, which meant that there was a build-up of fluid in his lungs that was literally drowning him. Jim's skin was dark blue and felt cold and clammy and he was blowing white frothy bubbles out through his lips with every laboured breath.

'You're going to feel much better soon, sir,' Jed said. The paramedics had already inserted an IV and as Jed ordered morphine and diuretics, Jasmine was already pulling up the drugs, but when she got a little lost on the trolley he pointed them out without the tutting and eye-rolls Penny had administered.

'Can you ring for a portable chest X-ray?' Jed asked. The radiographer would have just got back to her department as Jasmine went to summon her again.

'What's the number?' Jasmine asked, but then found it for herself on the phone pad.

Jed worked in a completely different manner from Penny. He was much calmer and far more polite with his requests and was patient when Jasmine couldn't find the catheter pack he asked for—he simply went and got one for himself. He apologised too when he asked the weary night radiographer to hold on for just a moment as he inserted a catheter. But, yes, Jasmine noticed, Vanessa was right—he was detached with the staff and nothing like the man she had mildly joked with at her interview or walked alongside on the beach.

But, like Penny, he got the job done.

Jasmine spoke reassuringly to Jim all the time and with oxygen on, a massive dose of diuretics and the calming effect of the morphine their patient's oxygen sats were slowly climbing and his skin was becoming pink. The terrified grip on Jasmine's hand loosened.

Lisa was as good as her word and popped in and out. Insisting she was done with her ovaries, she put on a lead gown and shooed them out for a moment and they stepped outside for the X-ray.

Strained was the silence and reluctantly almost, as if he was forcing himself to be polite, Jed turned his face towards her as they waited for the all-clear to go back inside. 'Enjoying your first day?'

'Actually, yes!' She was surprised at the enthusiasm in her answer as she'd been dreading starting work and

leaving Simon, and worried that her scrambled brain
wasn't up to a demanding job. Yet, less than an hour into
her first shift, Jasmine was realising how much she'd
missed it, how much she had actually loved her work.

'Told you it wouldn't take long.'

'Yes, well, I'm only two patients in.' She frowned as
he looked up, not into her eyes but at her hair. 'The hairdresser cut too much off.'

'No, no.' He shook his head. 'It's white.'

'Oh.' She shook it and a little puff of plaster dust
blew into the air. 'Plaster dust.' She shook it some more,
moaning at how she always ended up messy, and he
sort of changed his smile to a stern nod as the red light
flashed and then the radiographer called that they could
go back inside.

'You're looking better.' Jasmine smiled at her patient
because now the emergency was over, she could make
him a touch more comfortable. The morphine had kicked
in and his catheter bag was full as the fluid that had been
suffocating him was starting to move from his chest.
'How are you feeling?'

'Like I can breathe,' Jim said, and grabbed her hand,
still worried. 'Can my wife come in? She must've been
terrified.'

'I'm going to go and speak to her now,' Jed said, 'and
then I'll ring the medics to come and take over your care.
You're doing well.' He looked at Jasmine. 'Can you stay
with him while I go and speak to his wife?'

'Sure.'

'I thought that was it,' Jim admitted as Jasmine placed
some pillows behind him and put a blanket over the sheet
that covered him. After checking his obs, she sat her-

self down on the hard flat resus bed beside him. 'Libby thought so too.'

'Your wife?' Jasmine checked, and he nodded.

'She couldn't remember the number for the ambulance.'

'It must have been very scary for her,' Jasmine said, because though it must be terrifying to not be able to breathe, to watch someone you love suffer must have been hell. 'She'll be so pleased to see that you're talking and looking so much better than when you came in.'

Libby was pleased, even though she promptly burst into tears when she saw him, and it was Jim who had to reassure her, rather than the other way around.

They were the most gorgeous couple—Libby chatted enough for both of them and told Jasmine that they were about to celebrate their golden wedding anniversary, which was certainly an achievement when she herself hadn't even managed to make it to one year.

'I was just telling Jasmine,' Libby said when Jed came in to check on Jim's progress, 'that it's our golden wedding anniversary in a fortnight.'

'Congratulations.' Jed smiled.

'The children are throwing us a surprise party,' Libby said. 'Well, they're hardly children...'

'And it's hardly a surprise.' Jed smiled again. 'Are you not supposed to know about it?'

'No,' Libby admitted. 'Do you think that Jim will be okay?'

'He should be,' Jed said. 'For now I'm going to ring the medics and have them take over his care, but if he continues improving I would expect him to be home by the end of the week—and ready to *gently* celebrate by the next.'

They were such a lovely couple and Jasmine adored seeing their closeness, but more than that she really was enjoying being back at work and having her world made bigger instead of fretting about her own problems. She just loved the whole buzz of the place, in fact.

It was a nice morning, a busy morning, but the staff were really friendly and helpful—well, most of them. Penny was Penny and especially caustic when Jasmine missed a vein when she tried to insert an IV.

'I'll do it!' She snapped, 'the patient doesn't have time for you to practise on him.'

'Why don't you two go to lunch?' Lisa suggested as Jasmine bit down on her lip.

'She has such a lovely nature!' Vanessa nudged Jasmine as they walked round to the staffroom. 'Honestly, pay no attention to Penny. She's got the patience of a two-year-old and, believe me, I speak from experience when I say that they have none. How old is your son?' She must have the seen that Jasmine was a bit taken aback by her question, as she hadn't had time to mention Simon to Vanessa yet. 'I saw you dropping him off at crèche this morning when I was bringing in Liam.'

'Your two-year-old?'

'My terrible two-year-old,' Vanessa corrected as they went to the fridge and took out their lunches and Vanessa told her all about the behavioural problems she was having with Liam.

'He's completely adorable,' Vanessa said as they walked through to the staffroom, 'but, God, he's hard work.'

Jed was in the staffroom and it annoyed Jasmine that she even noticed—after all, there were about ten people in there, but it was him that she noticed and he was also the reason she blushed as Vanessa's questions became a bit more personal.

'No.' Jasmine answered when Vanessa none-too-subtly asked about Simon's father—but that was nursing, especially in Emergency. Everyone knew everything about everyone's life and not for the first time Jasmine wondered how she was supposed to keep the fact she was Penny's sister a secret.

'We broke up before he was born.'

'You poor thing,' Vanessa said, but Jasmine shook her head.

'Best thing,' she corrected.

'And does he help?' Vanessa pushed, 'with the childcare? Now that you're working...'

She could feel Jed was listening and she felt embarrassed. Embarrassed at the disaster her life was, but she tried not to let it show in her voice, especially as Penny had now walked in and was sitting in a chair on the other side of the room.

'No, he lives on the other side of the city. I just moved back here a few weeks ago.'

'Your family is here?' Vanessa checked.

'Yes.' Jasmine gave a tight smile and concentrated on her cheese sandwich, deciding that in future she would have lunch in the canteen.

'Well, it's good that you've got them to support you,' Vanessa rattled on, and Jasmine didn't even need to look at Penny to see that she wasn't paying any attention. Her sister was busy catching up on notes during her break. Penny simply didn't stop working, wherever she was. Penny had always been driven, though there had been one brief period where she'd softened a touch. She'd dated for a couple of years and had been engaged, but that had ended abruptly and since then all it had been was work, work, work.

Which was why Penny had got as far as she had, Jasmine knew, but sometimes, more than sometimes, she wished her sister would just slow down.

Thankfully the conversation shifted back to Vanessa's son, Liam—and she told Jasmine that she was on her own, too. Jasmine would have quite enjoyed learning all about her colleagues under normal circumstances but for some reason she was finding it hard to relax today.

And she knew it was because of Jed.

God, she so did not want to notice him, didn't want to be aware of him in any way other than as a colleague. She had enough going on in her life right now, but when Jed stood and stretched and yawned, she knew what that stomach looked like beneath the less than well-ironed shirt, knew just how nice he could be, even if he was ignoring her now. He opened his eyes and caught her looking at him and he almost frowned at her. As he looked away Jasmine found that her cheeks were on fire, but thankfully Vanessa broke the uncomfortable moment.

'Did you get called in last night?' Vanessa asked him.

'Nope,' Jed answered. 'Didn't sleep.'

Jed headed back out to the department and carried on. As a doctor he was more than used to working while he was tired but it was still an effort and at three-thirty Jed made a cup of strong coffee and took it back to the department with him, wishing he could just go home and crash, annoyed with himself over his sleepless night.

He'd had a phone call at eleven-thirty the previous night and, assuming it was work, had answered it without thinking.

Only to be met by silence.

He'd hung up and checked the number and had seen that it was *private*.

And then the phone had rung again.

'Jed Devlin.' He had listened to the silence and then hung up again and stared at the phone for a full ten minutes, waiting for it to ring again.

It had.

'Jed!' He heard the sound of laughter and partying and then the voice of Rick, an ex-colleague he had trained with. 'Jed, is that you?'

'Speaking.'

'Sorry, I've been trying to get through.'

'Where are you?'

'Singapore… What time is it there?'

'Coming up for midnight.'

'Sorry about that. I just found out that you moved to Melbourne.'

He had laughed and chatted and caught up with an old friend and it was nice to chat and find out what was going on in his friend's life and to congratulate him on the birth of his son, but twenty minutes later his heart was still thumping.

Two hours later he still wasn't asleep.

By four a.m. Jed realised that even if the past was over with, he himself wasn't.

And most disconcerting for Jed was the new nurse that had started today.

He had found it easy to stick to his self-imposed rule. He really wasn't interested in anyone at work and just distanced himself from all the fun and conversations that were so much a part of working in an emergency department.

Except he *had* noticed Jasmine.

From the second he'd seen her standing talking to Penny, all flustered and red-cheeked, her dark curls bobbing, and her blue eyes had turned to him, he'd noticed her in a way he'd tried very hard not to. When he'd heard she was applying for a job in Emergency, his guard had shot up, but he had felt immediate relief when he'd heard someone call her Mrs Phillips.

It had sounded pretty safe to him.

There had been no harm in being friendly, no chance of anything being misconstrued, because if she was a Mrs then he definitely wasn't interested, which meant there was nothing to worry about.

But it would seem now that there was.

'Thanks, Jed.' He turned to the sound of Jasmine's voice as she walked past him with Vanessa.

'For?'

'Your help today, especially with Jim. I had no idea where the catheter packs were. It's good to get through that first shift back.'

'Well, you survived it.' He gave a very brief nod and turned back to his work.

'More importantly, the patients did!' Jasmine called as she carried on walking with Vanessa.

They were both heading to the crèche, he guessed. He fought the urge to watch her walk away, not looking up until he heard the doors open and then finally snap closed.

Not that Jasmine noticed—she was more than used to moody doctors who changed like the wind. For now she was delighted that her first shift had ended and as she and Vanessa headed to the crèche, Jasmine realised she had made a friend.

'He's gorgeous!' Vanessa said as Jasmine scooped up Simon. 'He's so blond!'

He was—blond and gorgeous, Simon had won the staff over on *his* first day with his happy smile and his efforts to talk.

'This is Liam!' Vanessa said. He was cute too, with a mop of dark curls and a good dose of ADD in the making. Jasmine stood smiling, watching as Vanessa took about ten minutes just to get two shoes on her lively toddler.

'Thank goodness for work,' Vanessa groaned. 'It gives me a rest!'

'Don't look now,' Vanessa said as they walked out of the crèche, 'they're getting something big in.' Jed and Lisa were standing outside where police on motorbikes had gathered in the forecourt. Screens were being put up and for a moment Jasmine wondered if her first day was actually over or if they were going to be asked to put the little ones back into crèche.

'Go.' Lisa grinned as Vanessa checked what was happening. 'The screens are for the press—we have ourselves a celebrity arriving.'

'Who?' Vanessa asked.

'Watch the news.' Lisa winked. 'Go on, shoo...'

'Oh,' Jasmine grumbled, because she really wanted to know. She glanced at Jed, who looked totally bored with the proceedings, and there was really no chance of a sophisticated effort because Simon was bouncing up and down with excitement at the sight of police cars and Liam was making loud siren noises. 'I guess I'll have to tune in at six to find out.'

And that was the stupid thing about Emergency, Jasmine remembered.

You couldn't wait for the shift to finish—even today, as much as she'd enjoyed her shift, as soon as lunchtime had ended, she had been counting the minutes, desperate to get to the crèche and pick up Simon.

Except that the second she had finished her shift, she wanted to go back.

'I've missed it,' she told Vanessa as they walked to the car park. 'I was looking at a job in MRI, but I really do like working in Emergency.'

'I'm the same,' Vanessa admitted. 'I couldn't work anywhere else.'

'The late shifts are going to be the killer, though,' Jasmine groaned, 'and I don't even want to think about nights.'

'You'll work it out.' Vanessa said. 'I've got a lovely babysitter: Ruby. She's studying childcare, she goes to my church and she's always looking for work. And if she can deal with Liam she can more than handle Simon. She's got really strict parents so she loves spending evenings and sometimes nights at my place.' She gave Jasmine a nudge. 'Though I do believe her boyfriend might pop over at times. Just to study, of course…'

They both laughed.

It was nice to laugh, nice to be back at work and making friends.

Nice to sit down for dinner on the sofa, with a for-once-exhausted Simon. 'Come on,' Jasmine coaxed, but he wasn't interested in the chicken and potatoes she was feeding him and in the end Jasmine gave in and warmed up his favourite ready meal in the microwave. 'I'm not buying any more,' Jasmine warned as he happily tucked in, but Simon just grinned.

And it was nice to turn on the news and to actually feel like you had a little finger on the pulse of the world.

She listened to the solemn voice of the newsreader telling the viewers about a celebrity who was '*resting*' at the Peninsula after being found unconscious. She got a glimpse of Jed walking by the stretcher as it was wheeled in, holding a sheet over the unfortunate patient's face. Then Jasmine watched as Mr Dean spoke, saying the patient was being transferred to ICU and there would be no further comment from the hospital.

It wasn't exactly riveting, so why did she rewind the feature?

Why did she freeze the screen?

Not in the hope of a glimpse at the celebrity.

And certainly not so she could listen again to Mr Dean.

It was Jed's face she paused on and then changed her mind.

She was finished with anything remotely male, Jasmine reminded herself, and then turned as Simon, having finished his meal and bored with the news, started bobbing up and down in front of the television.

'Except you, little man.'

CHAPTER SIX

JED DID CONCENTRATE on work.

Absolutely.

He did his best to ignore Jasmine, or at least to speak to her as little as possible at work, and he even just nodded to her when they occasionally crossed paths at the local shop, or he would simply run past her and Simon the odd evening they were on the beach.

He was a funny little lad. He loved to toddle on the beach and build sandcastles, but Jed noticed that despite her best efforts, Jasmine could not get him into the water.

Even if he tried not to notice, Jed saw a lot as he ran along the stretch of sand—Jasmine would hold the little boy on her hip and walk slowly into the water, but Simon would climb like a cat higher up her hip until Jasmine would give in to his sobs and take him back to the dry sand.

'You get too tense.' He gave in after a couple of weeks of seeing this ritual repeated. He could see what Jasmine was doing wrong and even if he ignored her at work, it seemed rude just to run past and not stop and talk now and then.

'Sorry?' She'd given up trying to take Simon into the water a few moments ago and now they were patting a sandcastle into shape. She looked up when Jed stood over her and Jasmine frowned at his comment, but in a curious way rather than a cross one.

He concentrated on her frown, not because she was resting back on her heels to look up at him, not because she was wearing shorts and a bikini top, he just focused on her frown. 'When you try to get him to go into the water. I've seen you.' He grinned. 'You get tense even before you pick him up to take him in there.'

'Thanks for the tip.' Jasmine looked not at Jed but at Simon. 'I really want him to love the water. I was hoping by the end of summer he'd at least be paddling, but he starts screaming as soon as I even get close.'

'He'll soon get used to it just as soon as you relax.' And then realising he was sounding like an authority when he didn't have kids of his own, he clarified things a little. 'I used to be a lifeguard, so I've watched a lot of parents trying to get reluctant toddlers into the water.'

'A lifeguard!' Jasmine grinned. 'You're making me blush.'

She was funny. She wasn't pushy or flirty, just funny.

'That was a long time ago,' Jed said.

'A volunteer?'

'Nope, professional. I was paid—it put me through medical school.'

'So how should I be doing it?'

'I'll show you.' He offered her his hand and pulled her up and they walked towards the water's edge. 'Just sit here.'

'He won't come.'

'I bet he does if you ignore him.'

So they sat and chatted for ten minutes or so. Simon

grew bored, playing with his sandcastle alone, while the grown-ups didn't care that they were sitting in the water in shorts, getting wet with each shallow wave that came in.

Jed told her about his job, the one he'd had before medical school. 'It was actually that which made me want to work in emergency medicine,' Jed explained. 'I know you shouldn't enjoy a drowning...'

She smiled because she knew what he meant. There was a high that came from emergencies, just knowing that you knew what to do in a fraught situation.

Of course not all the time; sometimes it was just miserable all around, but she could see how the thrill of a successful resuscitation could soon plant the seeds for a career in Emergency.

'So if I drown, will you rescue me?'

'Sure,' Jed said, and her blue eyes turned to his and they smiled for a very brief moment. Unthinking, absolutely not thinking, he said it. 'Why? Is that a fantasy of yours?'

And he could have kicked himself, should have kicked himself, except she was just smiling and so too was he. Thankfully, starved of attention, Simon toddled towards them and squealed with delight at the feeling of water rushing past his feet.

'Yay!' Jasmine was delighted, taking his hands and pulling him in for a hug. 'It worked.'

'Glad to have helped.' Jed stood, because *now* he was kicking himself, now he was starting to wonder what might have happened had Simon not chosen that moment to take to the water.

Actually, he wasn't wondering.

Jed knew.

'Better get on.' He gave her a thin smile, ruffled Simon's hair and off down the beach he went, leaving Jasmine sitting there.

Jed confused her.

Cold one minute and not warm but hot the next.

And, no, being rescued by a sexy lifeguard wasn't one of her fantasies, but a sexy Jed?

Well…

She blew out a breath. There was something happening between them, something like she had never known before. Except all he did was confuse her—because the next time she saw him at work he went back to ignoring her.

As well as confusing, Jed was also wrong about her getting right back into the swing of things at work. The department was busy and even a couple weeks later she still felt like the new girl at times. Even worse, her mum was less than pleased when Lisa asked, at short notice, if Jasmine could do two weeks of nights. She had staff sick and had already moved Vanessa onto the roster to do nights. Jasmine understood the need for her to cover, but she wasn't sure her mum would be quite so understanding.

'I'm really sorry about this,' Jasmine said to her mum as she dropped Simon off.

'It's fine.' Louise had that rather pained, martyred look that tripped all of Jasmine's guilt switches. 'I've juggled a few clients' appointments to early evening for this week so I'll need you to be back here at five.'

'Sure.'

'But, Jasmine,' Louise said, 'how are you going to keep on doing this? I'm going away soon and if they can change your roster at five minutes' notice and expect you to comply, how are you going to manage?'

'I've a meeting with a babysitter at the weekend,' Jasmine told her mum. 'She's coming over and I'll see how she gets on with Simon.'

'How much is a babysitter going to cost?' Louise asked, and Jasmine chose not to answer, but really something would have to give.

Paying the crèche was bad enough, but by the time she'd paid a babysitter to pick Simon up for her late shifts and stints on nights, well, it was more complicated than Jasmine had the time to allocate it right now.

'How are things with Penny at work?' Louise asked.

'It seems okay.' Jasmine shrugged. 'She's just been on nights herself so I haven't seen much of her, and when I do she's no more horrible to me than she is to everybody else.'

'And no one's worked out that you're sisters?'

'How could they?' Jasmine said. 'Penny hasn't said anything and no one is going to hear it from me.'

'Well, make sure that they don't,' Louise warned. 'Penny doesn't need any stress right now. She's worked up enough as it is with this promotion coming up. Maybe once that's over with she'll come around to the idea a bit more.'

'I'd better get going.' Jasmine gave Simon a cuddle and held him just an extra bit tight.

'Are you okay?' Louise checked.

'I'm fine,' Jasmine said, but as she got to the car she remembered why she was feeling more than a little out of sorts. And, no, she hadn't shared it with her mum and certainly she wouldn't be ringing up Penny for a chat to sort out her feelings.

There on the driver's seat was her newly opened post and even though she'd been waiting for it, even though she wanted it, it felt strange to find out in such a banal way that she was now officially divorced.

Yes, she'd been looking forward to the glorious day, only the reality of it gave her no reason to smile.

Her marriage had been the biggest mistake of her life.

The one good thing to come out of it was Simon.

The *only* good thing, Jasmine thought, stuffing the papers into her glove box, and, not for the first time she felt angry.

She'd been duped so badly.

Completely lied to from the start.

Yes, she loved Simon with all her heart, but this was never the way she'd intended to raise a child. With a catalogue of crèches and babysitters and scraping to make ends meet and a father who, despite so many promises, when the truth had been exposed, when his smooth veneer had been cracked and the real Lloyd had surfaced, rather than facing himself had resumed the lie his life was and had turned his back and simply didn't want to know his own son.

'Are you okay?' Vanessa checked later as they headed out of the locker rooms.

'I'm fine,' Jasmine said, but hearing the tension in her own voice and realising she'd been slamming about a bit in the locker room, she conceded, 'My divorce just came through.'

'Yay!' said Vanessa, and it was a new friend she turned to rather than her family. 'You should be out celebrating instead of working.'

'I will,' Jasmine said. 'Just not yet.'

'Are you upset?'

'Not upset,' Jasmine said. 'Just angry.'

'Excuse me.' They stepped aside as a rather grumpy Dr Devlin brushed passed.

'Someone got out of the wrong side of bed,' Vanessa said.

Jasmine didn't get Jed.

She did not understand why he had changed so rapidly.

But he had.

From the nice guy she had met he was very brusque. *Very* brusque.

Not just to her, but to everyone. Still, Jasmine could be brusque too when she had to be, and on a busy night in Emergency, sometimes that was exactly what you had to be.

'You've done this before!' Greg, the charge nurse, grinned as Jasmine shooed a group of inebriated teenagers down to the waiting room. They were worried about their friend who'd been stabbed but were starting to fight amongst themselves.

'I used to be a bouncer at a night club.' Jasmine winked at her patient, who was being examined by Jed.

Greg laughed and even the patient smiled.

Jed just carried right on ignoring her.

Which was understandable perhaps, given that they were incredibly busy.

But what wasn't understandable to Jasmine was that he refused a piece of the massive hazelnut chocolate bar she opened at about one a.m., when everyone else fell on it.

Who doesn't like chocolate? Jasmine thought as he drank water.

Maybe he was worried about his figure?

He stood outside the cubicle now, writing up the card. 'Check his pedal pulses every fifteen minutes.' He thrust her a card and she read his instructions.

'What about analgesia?' Jasmine checked.

'I've written him up for pethidine.'

'No.' Jasmine glanced down at the card. 'You haven't.'

Jed took the card from her and rubbed his hand over his unshaven chin, and Jasmine tried to tell herself that he had his razor set that way, that he cultivated the unshaven, up-all-night, just-got-out-of-bed look, that this man's looks were no accident.

Except he had been up all night.

Jed let out an irritated hiss as he read through the patient's treatment card, as if she were the one who had made the simple mistake, and then wrote up the prescription in his messy scrawl.

'Thank you!' Jasmine smiled sweetly—just to annoy him.

She didn't get a smile back.

Mind you, the place was too busy to worry about Jed's bad mood and brooding good looks, which seemed to get more brooding with every hour that passed.

At six a.m., just as things were starting to calm down, just as they were starting to catch up and tidy the place for the day staff, Jasmine found out just how hard this job could be at times.

Found, just as she was starting to maybe get into the swing of things, that perhaps this wasn't the place she really wanted to be after all.

They were alerted that a two-week-old paediatric arrest was on his way in but the ambulance had arrived before they had even put the emergency call out.

Jasmine took the hysterical parents into an interview room and tried to get any details as best she could as the overhead loudspeaker went off, urgently summoning the paediatric crash team to Emergency. It played loudly in the interview room also, each chime echoing the urgency, and there was the sound of footsteps running and doors slamming, adding to the parents' fear.

'The doctors are all with your baby,' Jasmine said. 'Let them do their work.' Cathy, the new mum, still looked pregnant. She kept saying she had only had him two weeks and that this couldn't be happening, that she'd taken him out of his crib and brought him back to bed, and when the alarm had gone off for her husband to go to work... And then the sobbing would start again.

She kept trying to push past Jasmine to get to her baby, but eventually she collapsed into a chair and sobbed with her husband that she just wanted to know what was going on.

'As soon as there's some news, someone will be in.' There was a knock at the door and she saw a policeman and -woman standing there. Jasmine excused herself, went outside and closed the door so she could speak to them.

'How are they?' the policewoman asked.

'Not great,' Jasmine said. 'A doctor hasn't spoken to them yet.'

'How are things looking for the baby?'

'Not great either,' Jasmine said. 'I really don't know much, though, I've just been in with the parents. I'm going to go and try to find out for them what's happening.' Though she was pretty sure she knew. One look at the tiny infant as he had arrived and her heart had sunk.

'Everything okay?' Lisa, early as always, was just coming on duty and she came straight over.

'We've got a two-week-old who's been brought in in full arrest,' Jasmine explained. 'I was just going to try and get an update for the parents.'

'Okay.' Lisa nodded. 'You do that and I'll stay with them.'

Jasmine wasn't sure what was worse, sitting in with the hysterical, terrified parents or walking into Resus and hearing the silence as they paused the resuscitation for a moment to see if there was any response.

There was none.

Jed put his two fingers back onto the baby's chest and started the massage again, but the paediatrician shook his head.

'I'm calling it.'

It was six twenty-five and the paediatrician's voice was assertive.

'We're not going to get him back.'

He was absolutely right—the parents had started the resuscitation and the paramedics had continued it for the last thirty-five futile minutes. Jasmine, who would normally have shed a tear at this point before bracing herself to face the family, just stood frozen.

Vanessa cried. Not loudly. She took some hand wipes from the dispenser and blew her nose and Jed took his fingers off the little infant and sort of held his nose between thumb and finger for a second.

It was a horrible place to be.

'Are you okay?' Greg looked over at Jasmine and she

gave a short nod. She dared not cry, even a little, because if she started she thought she might not stop.

It was the first paediatric death she had dealt with since she'd had Simon and she was shocked at her own reaction. She just couldn't stop looking at the tiny scrap of a thing and comparing him to her own child, and how the parents must be feeling. She jumped when she heard the sharp trill of a pager.

'Sorry.' The paediatrician looked down at his pager. 'I'm needed urgently on NICU.'

'Jed, can you…?'

Jed nodded as he accepted the grim task. 'I'll tell the parents.'

'Thanks, and tell them that I'll come back down and talk to them at length as soon as I can.'

'Who's been dealing with the parents?' Jed asked when the paediatrician had gone.

'Me,' Jasmine said. 'Lisa's in there with them now. The police are here as well.'

'I'll speak first to the parents,' Jed said. 'Probably just keep it with Lisa. She'll be dealing with them all day.'

Jasmine nodded. 'They wanted a chaplain.' She could hear the police walkie-talkies outside and her heart ached for the parents, not just for the terrible news but having to go over and over it, not only with family but with doctors and the police, and for all that was to come.

'I'll go and ring the chaplain,' Greg said. 'And I'd better write up the drugs now.' He looked at the chaos. There were vials and wrappers everywhere, all the drawers on the trolley were open. They really had tried everything, but all to no avail.

'I'll sort out the baby,' Vanessa said, and Jasmine,

who had never shied away from anything before, was relieved that she wouldn't have to deal with him.

'I'll restock,' Jasmine said.

Which was as essential as the other two things, Jasmine told herself as she started to tidy up, because you never knew what was coming through the door. The day staff were arriving and things needed to be left in order.

Except Jasmine *was* hiding and deep down she knew it, had been so relieved when Jed had suggested keeping things with Lisa. She screwed her eyes closed as screams carried through the department. Jed must have broken the news.

She just wanted to go home to her own baby, could not stand to think of their grief.

'Are you okay, Jasmine?' Vanessa asked as she stocked her trolley to take into Resus, preparing to wash and dress the baby so that his parents could hold him.

'I'll get there.' She just wanted the shift to be over, to ring her mum and check that Simon was okay, for the past hour not to have happened, because it wasn't fair, it simply was not fair. But of course patients kept coming in with headaches and chest pains and toothaches and there was still the crash trolley to restock and plenty of work to do.

And now here was Penny, all crisp and ready for work.

'Morning!' She smiled and no one really returned it. 'Bad night?' she asked Jed, who, having told the parents and spoken to the police, was admitting another patient.

'We just had a neonatal death,' Jed said. 'Two weeks old.'

'God.' Penny closed her eyes. 'How are the parents?'

'The paediatrician is in there with them now,' Jed

said. Jasmine was restocking the trolley, trying not to listen, just trying to tick everything off her list. 'But they're beside themselves, of course,' Jed said. 'Beautiful baby,' he added.

'Any ideas as to why?' Penny asked.

'It looks, at this stage, like an accidental overlay. Mum brought baby back to bed and fell asleep feeding him, Dad woke up to go to work and found him.'

She heard them discussing what had happened and heard Lisa come in and ask Vanessa if the baby was ready, because she wanted to take him into his parents. She didn't turn around, she didn't want to risk seeing him, so instead Jasmine just kept restocking the drugs they had used and the needles and wrappers and tiny little ET tubes and trying, and failing, to find a replacement flask of paediatric sodium bicarbonate that had been used in the resuscitation. Then she heard Penny's voice…

'The guidelines now say not to co-sleep.'

And it wasn't because it was Penny that the words riled Jasmine so much, or was it?

No.

It was just the wrong words at the wrong time.

'Guidelines?' Jasmine had heard enough, could not stand to hear Penny's cool analysis, and swung around. 'Where are the guidelines at three in the morning when you haven't slept all night and your new baby's screaming? Where are the guidelines when—?'

'You need to calm down, Nurse,' Penny warned.

That just infuriated Jasmine even more. 'It's been a long night. I don't feel particularly calm,' Jasmine retorted. 'Those parents have to live with this, have to live with not adhering to the *guidelines*, when they were simply doing what parents have done for centuries.'

Jasmine marched off to the IV room and swiped her ID card to get in, anger fizzing inside her, not just towards her sister but towards the world that was now minus that beautiful baby, and for all the pain and the grief the parents would face. Would she have said that if Penny hadn't been her sister?

The fact was, she *would* have said it, and probably a whole lot more.

Yes, Penny was right.

And the guidelines were right too.

But it was just so unfair.

She still couldn't find the paediatric sodium bicarbonate solution and rummaged through the racks because it had to be there, or maybe she should ring the children's ward and ask if they had some till pharmacy was delivered.

Then she heard the door swipe and Jed came in.

He was good like that, often setting up his drips and things himself. 'Are you okay?'

'Great!' she said through gritted teeth.

'I know that Penny comes across as unfeeling,' Jed said, 'but we all deal with this sort of thing in different ways.'

'I know we do.' Jasmine climbed up onto a stool, trying to find the IV flask. She so did not need the grief speech right now, did not need the debrief that was supposed to solve everything, that made things manageable, did not really want the world to be put into perspective just yet.

'She was just going through the thought process,' Jed continued.

'I get it.'

He could hear her angrily moving things, hear the upset in her voice, and maybe he should get Lisa to speak to her, except Lisa was busy with the parents right now and Greg was checking drugs and handing over to the day staff. Still, the staff looked out for each other in cases like this, and so that was what Jed did.

Or tried to.

'Jasmine, why don't you go and get a coffee and…?' He decided against suggesting that it might calm her down.

'I'm just finishing stocking up and then I'm going home.'

'Not yet. Look—' he was very patient and practical '—you're clearly upset.'

'Please.' Jasmine put up her hand. 'I really don't need to hear it.'

'I think you do,' Jed said.

'From whom?'

'Excuse me?' He clearly had no idea what she was alluding to, but there was a bubble of anger that was dangerously close to popping now, not just for this morning's terrible events but for the weeks of confusion, for the man who could be nice one minute and cool and distant the next, and she wanted to know which one she was dealing with.

'Am I being lectured to by Dr Devlin, or am I being spoken to by Jed?'

'I have no idea what you're talking about. You're distressed.' He knew exactly what she was talking about, knew exactly what she meant, yet of course he could not tell her that. Jed also knew he was handling this terribly, that fifteen minutes sitting in the staffroom being debriefed by him wasn't going to help either of them.

'I'm not distressed.'

'Perhaps not, but I think it would be very silly to leave like this. It would be extremely irresponsible to get into a car and drive home right now, so I'm suggesting that you go to the staffroom and sit down for fifteen minutes.' She stood there furious as she was being told what to do, not asked, she knew that.

'Fine.' She gave a terse smile. 'I will have a coffee and then I'll go home, but first I have to put this back on the crash trolley and order some more from pharmacy.'

'Do that, and then I'll be around shortly to talk to you.' Jed said, 'Look, I know it's hard, especially with one so young. It affects all of us in different ways. I know that I'm upset…'

She didn't say it, but the roll of her eyes as he spoke told him he couldn't possibly know, couldn't possibly understand how she felt.

'Oh, I get it,' Jed said. 'I can't be upset, I don't really get it, do I? Because I don't have a child, I couldn't possibly be as devastated as you.' His voice was rising, his own well-restrained anger at this morning's events starting to build. 'I'm just the machine that walks in and tells the parents that their baby's dead. What the hell would I know?'

'I didn't mean that.' She knew then that she was being selfish in her upset, but grief was a selfish place and one not easy to share.

'Oh, but I think you did,' Jed said. 'I think you meant exactly that.'

And he was right, she had, except that wasn't fair on either of them, because she had cried many times over a lost baby, it just felt different somehow when you had one at home. There was a mixture of guilt and pain tempered with shameful relief that it hadn't happened to her, because, yes, she'd taken Simon into bed with her, despite what the guidelines might say, and it wasn't fair on anyone.

It simply wasn't fair.

Jasmine had no idea how the next part happened. Later she would be tempted to ring Security and ask if she could review the security footage in treatment room two between seven twenty and seven twenty-five, because she'd finally located the sodium bicarbonate and stepped down from the stool and stood facing him, ready to row, both of them ready to argue their point, and the next moment she was being kissed to within an inch of her life.

Or was it the other way around?

She had no way of knowing who had initiated it, all she was certain of was that neither tried to stop it.

It was an angry, out-of-control kiss.

His chin was rough and dragged on her skin, and his tongue was fierce and probing. He tasted of a mixture of peppermint and coffee and she probably tasted of instant tomato soup or salty tears, but it was like no other kiss she had known.

It was violent.

She heard the clatter of a trolley that moved as they did.

It was a kiss that came with no warning and rapidly escalated.

It was a kiss that was completely out of bounds and out of hand.

She was pressed into the wall and Jed was pressing

into her; his hands were everywhere and so too were hers; she could feel his erection pressing into her. More than that she too was pushing herself up against him, her hands just as urgent as his, pulling his face into hers, and never had she lost control so quickly, never had she been more unaware of her surroundings because only the crackle of the intercom above reminded them of their location—only that, or shamefully she knew it could have gone further. Somehow they stopped themselves, somehow they halted it, except they were still holding each other's heads.

'And you thought driving would be careless and irresponsible,' Jasmine said.

He sort of blew out his breath. 'Jasmine…' He was right on the edge here, Jed realised, shocked at himself. 'I apologise.'

'No need to apologise,' Jasmine said. 'Or should I?'

'Of course not.' His mouth was there, right there, they were holding each other, restraining the other, and both still dangerously close to resuming what they mustn't. She could hear their breathing, fast and ragged and fighting to slow, and slowly too they let go of each other.

Her blouse was undone, just one button, and she didn't really know how, but he looked away as she did it up and moved away from him to pick up the flask she had dropped. She left him setting up his IV and went to head back out, but she could still taste him, was still not thinking straight. And then Lisa came in.

'Shouldn't you be heading home?'

'I couldn't find the paediatric sodium bicarb,' Jasmine said. 'There's only one left after this.'

'Thanks,' Lisa said. 'I'll get Joan to add it to the pharmacy order. Thanks for everything, Jasmine. I know that can't have been an easy shift.'

'How are the parents?'

'They're spending some time with him. The hospital chaplain is in with them and the police have been lovely.' Lisa looked at Jasmine. 'Maybe go and get a coffee before you go home.'

'I think I just want my bed,' Jasmine admitted. 'I just need to finish the crash trolley off and order some more of this.'

'I'll do that.' Lisa took the flask from her and they stepped aside as Jed walked past with his IV trolley. Very deliberately, neither met the other's eye.

'You go to bed and get a well-earned rest,' Lisa said.

Fat chance of that.

Jasmine did have a cup of coffee before she drove home.

Except she certainly wasn't hanging around to see Jed. Instead, she chose to head to the kiosk and get a takeaway.

And, of course, on the way to her car, she rang her mum.

'How was Simon last night?' Jasmine asked the second her mum answered.

'Fantastic. I haven't heard a peep out of him.'

'He's not up yet?'

'No, but he didn't go down to sleep till quite late.'

'You've checked him, though?' Jasmine could hear the anxiety in her voice

'I checked him before I went to bed. Jasmine, it's eight a.m. Surely it's good if he's having a little lie-in when he often has to be up at six for crèche?'

'Mum…'

She heard her mother's weary sigh as she walked through the house and then silence for a moment. She was being ridiculous, but even so, she needed the reassurance.

'He's asleep,' her mum said, 'and, yes, he's breathing.'

'Thank you.'

'Bad night?'

'Bad morning.'

'I'm sorry.' And then Louise started to laugh. 'He's just woken up—can you hear him?'

Jasmine smiled at the lovely morning sounds Simon made, calling out to anyone who was there, but she was dangerously close to tears a second later as she realised again just how lucky she was.

'Go and have a nice sleep and I'll see you here for dinner.'

'Thanks, Mum.'

Her mum could be so nice, Jasmine mused as she drove home. When she had Simon she was wonderful with him. Jasmine completely understood that her mother didn't want to be a permanent babysitter and she decided that when she woke up she *was* going to ring Ruby, Vanessa's babysitter, and maybe get together and see if they could work something out.

All the drive home she thought very practical thoughts, aware she was a little bit more than tired.

And upset.

And confused.

She parked in the carport and looked over at the beach, wondered if a walk might be soothing, but knowing her luck Jed would be running there soon and another encounter with him was the last thing either of them needed now.

So she showered and tried to block out the day with her blinds, set her alarm and did her level best not to think of those poor parents and what they were doing right now, but even trying not to think about them made her cry.

And it made her cry too, that she had been here twelve weeks now and Simon's father hadn't even rung once to see how he was, neither had he responded to the occasional photo of his son she sent him.

And then she got to the confusing part and she wasn't crying now as she went over the latter part of her shift.

Instead she was cringing as her mind wandered to a man who at every turn bemused her, and then to the kiss that they had shared.

She hadn't been kissed like that, ever.

Their response to each other's kiss had been so immediate, so consuming that, really, had the intercom not gone off, they'd have been unstoppable, and she burnt in embarrassment at the thought of what Lisa might have come in and found.

And she burnt, too, because in truth it was a side to him she had known was there—something she had felt the second he had jogged up to her on the beach. Jed was the first man to move her in a very long time, but she had never thought her feelings might be reciprocated, had never expected the ferocity of that kiss.

And she'd do very well to forget about it!

They had both been upset, Jasmine decided.

Angry.

Over-emotional.

It had been a one-off. She turned over and very deliberately closed her eyes. Yes, it would be a bit awkward facing him tonight but, hell, she'd faced worse.

She'd just pretend it had never happened.

And no doubt so would he.

She had her whole life to sort out without confusing things further.

And a man like Jed Devlin could only do that.

CHAPTER SEVEN

'MUM!' SIMON SAID it more clearly than he ever had before, and Jasmine scooped him up and cuddled him in tight the second she got to her mum's.

'You're early,' Louise commented. 'I said you didn't need to be here till five.'

'I didn't sleep very well,' Jasmine admitted. 'I'm going to go shopping at the weekend for some decent blinds.' Not that that was the entire reason! 'How has he been?'

'Okay. He's been asking after you a lot,' Louise said, when Jasmine rather wished that she wouldn't as she already felt guilty enough. 'Right, I'd better get ready.'

Louise appeared a little while later in a smart navy suit, with heels and make-up, looking every bit the professional real estate agent. 'How did you do it Mum?' Jasmine asked. 'I mean, you had evening appointments when we were little.'

'You were older than Simon when your dad left,' Louise pointed out. 'Penny's a good bit older than you and she was born sensible—I used to ask the neighbour to listen out for you. It was different times then,' she admitted.

Maybe, but nothing was going to fill the well of guilt

Jasmine felt leaving Simon so much and it was only going to get more complicated for him when she added a babysitter to the mix.

Still, she did her best not to worry about next week or next month, just concentrated on giving him his dinner, and when he spat it out she headed to her mum's freezer and, yes, there were chicken nuggets. He could eat them till he was eighteen, Jasmine thought, and let go of worrying about the small stuff for five minutes, just enjoyed giving him his bath and settling him, and then got herself ready for work.

There really wasn't time to stress about facing Jed, especially when her mum didn't get back till after eight, and by the time she raced into work the clock was already nudging nine but, of course, he was one of the first people she saw.

It was a bit awkward but actually not as bad as she'd feared.

As she headed to the lockers Jasmine met him in the corridor and screwed up her face as she blushed and mouthed the word, 'Sorry.'

'Me too,' Jed said, and possibly he too was blushing just a little bit.

'Upset, you know,' Jasmine said.

'I get it.'

'So it's forgotten?' Jasmine checked.

'Forgotten,' he agreed.

Except it wasn't quite so easy to forget a kiss like that, Jasmine knew, because through a restless sleep she had tried.

So too had Jed.

He was a master at self-recrimination, had been furious with himself all day, and that evening, getting ready for work, he'd braced himself to face her, to be cool and aloof, yet her blush and her grin and her 'sorry' had side-swiped him—had actually made him laugh just a little bit on the inside.

'I got you a present.' Vanessa smiled as, still blushing, Jasmine walked into the locker room and peered into the bag being handed to her. It was a bottle with ribbons tied to the neck. 'I think it should be real champagne, but sparkling wine will have to do. You can open it when you're ready to celebrate.'

'Thank you!' Jasmine was touched. 'I'll have a drink at the weekend.'

'I mean properly celebrate.' Vanessa winked. 'You can't pop that cork till…'

'It will be vintage by then.' Jasmine grinned.

It was a very different night from the one before.

It was quiet and the staff took advantage. Greg, the charge nurse, put some music on at the work station and when at four a.m. there were only a few patients waiting for beds or obs, instead of telling them to restock or reorder, he opened a book as Jasmine and Vanessa checked each other's blood sugars. They were low enough to merit another trip to the vending machine, they decided. Then they came back and checked each other's BP.

'It's so low!' Vanessa pulled a face as she unwrapped the cuff and Jasmine grinned, proud of herself for keeping her pulse and blood pressure down, with Jed sitting at the station.

He noticed how easily she laughed.

She noticed him, full stop.

Noticed that this time when she cracked open her chocolate he took a piece.

'Do you want your blood pressure checked, Jed?' Vanessa asked.

'No, thanks.'

Vanessa pulled a face at his grumpy tone. 'Do you work on it, Jed?' It was ten past four, well into the witching hour for night nurses, a quiet night, lights blazing, the humour becoming more wicked. 'Do you work on being all silent and moody?'

'No,' he said. 'I just work.'

'And that beard you're growing,' Vanessa pushed as Greg looked up and grinned, 'is it designer stubble?'

'No,' Jed said patiently. 'I went for a run when I got in from work and I was too tired to shave afterwards, and then I overslept.'

'You're sure about that?' Vanessa said. 'You're sure you're not a male model on the side?'

Jed had forgotten those times of late. He hadn't partaken in chit-chat and fun for a very long time, he'd been too busy concentrating only on work. Maybe he needed a coffee, maybe *his* blood sugar was down, because he was kind of remembering the harmless fun he had once had at work before it had all become a nightmare.

He sat there recalling the laughs that had been part of the job and he was almost smiling as Vanessa chatted on. There was such a difference between playing and flirting. Jed had always known that, he'd just forgotten how to mix the two of late, had lost one for fear of the other, but the atmosphere tonight was kind of bringing it back.

'When you go to the hairdresser's, do you ask them to leave that bit of fringe?' Vanessa teased. 'Just so it can fall over your eye?'

As he turned, Jasmine waited for a frown, for a sharp word, for a brusque put-down, but her smirking grin turned to a delighted one as he flopped his fringe forward, pouted his lips and looked over their shoulders in a haughty model pose.

And then as they screamed in laughter and even Greg did too, Jed got back to his notes.

Enough fun for one night, Jed told himself.

Except he'd set them off and now they were walking like models.

Greg was joining in too as he filled in the board, standing with one hand on his hip and talking in deliberately effeminate tones. Jed tried not to smile, not notice as he usually managed to—he had just blocked out this side of Emergency, had chosen to ignore the black humour and frivolity that sometimes descended.

And yet somehow it was coming back.

Somehow he was starting to remember that it wasn't all just about work.

And Jed knew why.

It was just that he didn't want to know why.

'I'm going for a sleep.' He stood. 'Call me if anything comes in or at six if it stays quiet.'

He could hear them laughing as he tried to rest.

And whatever they were doing it must be funny because he even heard the po-faced nursing supervisor, who must be doing her rounds, start to laugh.

Jed turned on the white noise machine but still he couldn't sleep.

He could do without this!

'Morning, sunshine!' Greg rapped on the door at six, but Jed was awake. He rolled out of bed and brushed his teeth, headed out, took a few bloods and discharged a couple of patients, and wished the place would pick up.

He got one query appendicitis and one very grumpy old man called Ken Jones. He had a chronically infected leg ulcer, which was being dressed by a visiting nurse twice a week, but he had decided at five-thirty a.m. that it was time to do something about it and had called an ambulance. He was very grubby and unkempt and had his radio with him, which was tuned in to a chat show.

'What's his blood sugar?'

'Eight,' Jasmine said.

'You're taking all your diabetic medication, Ken?' Jed checked.

'I just do what I'm told.'

'Okay.' Jed had already carefully examined the man and his leg and he chatted to him for a little while. 'I'm going to get the medics to come down and have a look at you,' Jed said, 'but it might take a while. We're really quiet down here but I know they're very busy up on the ward, so you might have to stay with us for a while. And we could look at the dressings nurse to come and have a good look at your wound and maybe try something new.'

'Up to you.'

'It could be a few hours,' Jed said.

'I don't make a fuss.'

Jed grinned as he walked out. 'He'll be ringing up the radio station to complain about how long he has to wait soon.'

'Does he really need to see the medics?'

'Probably not,' Jed said. 'Penny will probably clear him out by eight, but…' he gave a shrug, '…the old boy's lonely, isn't he? Anyway, he could do with a good looking over, his chest is a bit rattly and he's a bit dry. I'll run some bloods.'

'I'll order him breakfast,' Jasmine yawned.

She ordered a breakfast from the canteen and then checked on the query appendicitis. His drip was about through so she headed over to the IV room. When she swiped her card and saw that Jed was in there, sorting out his trolley to take the bloods, she nearly turned and ran.

But that would be making a big deal of things so instead she stepped in.

'We need to talk,' Jed said without looking up from his task.

'No we don't,' Jasmine said. 'Really, it's fine.'

'Sure about that?' Jed said, and then looked over.

And, no, she wasn't sure about that because the ghost of their kiss was there in the room. She could see the exact spot where he'd pressed her to the wall, feel again every feeling she had yesterday—except the anger, except the upset.

'What about we meet for coffee after work?' he suggested.

'People will see,' Jasmine said. 'You know what this place is like.' She certainly didn't want a hint of this getting back to Penny.

'I meant away from the hospital. Just to talk.'

She shook her head. She'd hardly slept yesterday and had to work tonight as well as stop by her mum's at five and give Simon his dinner.

'I just want to go to bed.' She opened her mouth to correct herself and thankfully they both actually laughed.

'I really,' Jasmine said slowly, 'and I mean *really* am in no position to start something. I know people say that, but I've got a whole lot of things to sort out before...' She shook her head. 'I'm not going there.'

'I get that,' Jed said. 'Believe me, I had no intention of getting involved with someone at work but yesterday, hell, these past weeks...' He wondered how something he had spent all yesterday regretting should be something he would happily do again right this minute.

'Is that why you've been so horrible?'

'I haven't,' he said, then conceded, 'Maybe a bit. We need to talk, maybe clear the air—because if we don't—'

'If we don't,' Jasmine interrupted, 'we're going to be caught making out in the IV cupboard.' She gave him a grin. 'And I have no intention of going there again.'

Except she was lying.

She was looking at his mouth as she said it.

And he was looking at hers.

Had Greg not come in, that was exactly what would have happened and they both knew it.

Yes, the air needed clearing.

CHAPTER EIGHT

'WHY IS HE waiting for the medics?'

Despite not having to start till eight, Penny was in at a quarter to seven, standing and staring at the admission board and determined to make the most of a rare opportunity to clear the board and start her working day with not a single patient.

'He's brewing something.' Jed shrugged.

'We're not a holding pen,' Penny said. 'I'll get the nurses to order him transport home.'

'Let him have his breakfast at least.'

'Of course he can have his breakfast—by the time transport gets here he'll probably have had lunch as well.' She glanced briefly at a weary Jed. 'You look awful.'

'It's easier when it's busy,' Jed yawned.

'Go home,' she said.

'I might just do that.' And then he looked at Penny, who was rather determinedly not turning round to face him, just staring fixedly at the board. 'Speaking of looking awful...' he waited till she reluctantly turned to face him and he saw her red swollen eye '...what happened?'

'I walked into a branch.'

'Ouch.' Jasmine walked over just as he was taking a look.

'Ooh.' She winced when she saw Penny's red eye. 'Penny, what happened?' And then she remembered she wasn't supposed to be her sister.

'My neighbour's tree overhangs,' she said darkly. 'Though it won't by the time I get home—I've left them a note, telling them what's happened and that they'd better cut it.'

Jasmine could just imagine she had, and what was in it. And she could picture the branch, too, and Penny's gorgeous old neighbours who would be so upset.

Trust Penny to handle things so sensitively!

Of course she said nothing.

'I'll have a look,' Jed said, and went to buzz Reception to get Penny an admission card.

'I don't need to be registered,' Penny snapped. 'It's just a scratch.'

'A nasty scratch on your cornea,' Jed confirmed a few minutes later. Penny was sitting at the nurses' station and Jed had put some fluorescein drops into her eye. It made her eye bright yellow but any scratches showed up green. 'You need antibiotic drops and to keep it covered. When was your last tetanus booster?'

'I can't remember,' Penny said. 'I'm sure I'm up to date.'

'Penny?' Jed checked, as Jasmine walked in.

'Ken Jones just spiked a temp—his temp's thirty-eight point nine.'

'I'll do cultures.' Jed grinned, and Penny rolled her tongue in her cheek because now the old boy would have to be admitted.

'I'll do them,' she sighed.

'Not yet,' Jed yawned. 'I'll just give you your tetanus shot.'

'I'll go to my GP.'

'Don't be ridiculous,' Jed said, already opening a trolley and pulling out a syringe.

It was then that Jasmine *had* to say something.

'I'll do that.' Jasmine smiled. 'You can do the cultures.'

'I'll do the cultures,' Penny said. 'You go home, Jed, and think about shaving.'

Jasmine said nothing, not a single word as they headed into a cubicle and Penny unbuttoned her blouse. She just handed her a wad of tissues as Penny started crying.

Penny was, as Jasmine knew only too well, petrified of needles.

Not a little bit scared, completely petrified of them, though she didn't blink when sticking them in others.

'If you breathe a word of this...'

She was shaking on the seat as Jasmine swabbed her arm.

'No, wait!' Penny said.

'For what?' Jasmine said, sticking the needle in. 'Done.' She smiled at her. 'You big baby.'

'I know, I know.' Penny shuddered. 'Just give me a minute, would you? Go and set up for those blood cultures.' She had snapped straight back to being Penny, except this time Jasmine was smiling.

Jed didn't think about shaving.

He had a shower and tried not to think about Jasmine.

And then he pulled on some running clothes and ran

the length of the beach and told himself to just concentrate on work.

Only this time it didn't work.

And he saw where she lived and her car pull up in her carport and he saw Jasmine minus an armful of Simon but holding a bottle of champagne, which confused him, and he tried to continue to run.

What on earth was he going to say to her if he knocked at her door?

At least nothing would happen, he consoled himself, as ten minutes later he found himself doing just that, because given he wasn't exactly fresh out of the shower, there would be no repeats of yesterday.

Except *she* was fresh out of the shower when she opened the door and he prided himself on the fact that he did not look down, that he somehow held her eyes, even though her dressing gown did little to hide her womanly shape.

'Bad timing?'

'A bit.'

'Well, I won't keep you from your champagne.' He didn't want to make her laugh, except he did so, only he wasn't here for that.

'It's in the fridge.'

'Good.'

'A present.'

'That's nice.'

'Well?' Jasmine demanded. 'Which Jed am I talking to this morning?' And she looked at him standing there, and she knew who it was—the beachside Jed, the man who made her smile, the Jed who had made his first appearance at work just a few hours ago.

'I like to keep my work and personal life separate,'

he offered as way of an explanation, only it didn't wash with Jasmine. Penny did too but she was a cow both in and out of work. Yet with Jed sometimes she felt as if she was dealing with two completely different people.

But she liked this one.

Really liked this one, and, no, maybe they weren't going anywhere, maybe it was just all a bit much for him, she was a mother to one year old after all, but that he was here, that at this hour of the morning he stood at her door, when sensible shift workers should be firmly asleep, proved the undeniable attraction.

'I just wanted to say that I am really sorry and that it won't happen again. There'll be no more inappropriateness.'

'And it won't happen again at this end,' Jasmine said. 'Nothing inappropriate…'

Jed nodded and turned to go, except she didn't want him to. She was tired of running from the past, tired of saving for the future—she just wanted a little bit of living for now.

'At least, not at work.'

And for two years Jed had kept things separate. Despite some temptations, he had kept fiercely to his rule.

But Jed's rules had never been tested at this level.

Had they not kissed yesterday he might have been able to walk away.

Had he not tasted lips that were exactly suited to his, he might have headed back to the beach and then home.

But more than that, her blush and eye roll and 'sorry' last night, her total lack of pursuit or demands meant more to Jed than Jasmine could possibly know.

Bottom line?

They wanted each other.

Not a little bit of want, it was a morning after a sleepless nights want. It was twenty-five hours since yesterday's kiss and for twenty-five hours it had been on both of their minds.

He walked into the hallway and his mouth met hers.

And his chin was even rougher than yesterday.

And yesterday, though their kiss had been fierce it had been tempered on both sides with bitter restraint.

But now they could have what they wanted.

Each other.

For now, at least, it could be as simple as that.

She didn't care that he was damp from running. He smelt fresh and male and she knew what was under that T-shirt, and as she pulled it up and over his head she didn't just get to glimpse, she got to feel, and, no, he wasn't annoyed at the intrusion this time.

He tugged at her dressing gown as his mouth was everywhere—on her lips, on her neck and on her breasts. Meanwhile, she pulled at his shorts, because he was pressed so hard into her, and they pulled apart just enough to get to the bedroom—they weren't in the treatment room now and they quickly celebrated the fact.

She wanted to see what she had felt and she manoeuvred his shorts and all things unnecessary and he kicked off his running shoes and stepped out of them and they were naked in seconds, and seconds from impact.

'Condoms.' She was on the floor, going through his shorts.

'I don't run with them.' Jed laughed.

She was at eye level with his crotch as she knelt up and pressed her lips to him, pleased with a brief taste. Too selfish to continue, she dashed to her tiny bathroom and pulled the cupboard under the sink apart for condoms that were somewhere in a box she hadn't sorted in ages.

She was uncaring as Jed watched her bottom sticking up as she searched in the cupboard and her breasts jiggling as she turned round and it was safer that he go back into the bedroom.

Oh, my.

It was all Jasmine could think as she walked back towards him, because he was better than anything she had fashioned in her mind. He was incredibly fit and toned. She should have been shy as she walked over, but shy was the furthest thing from her mind and anyway, he didn't wait for her to finish walking—both of them were happy to collide.

He was just so into her body, so wanting, and he didn't need to worry about speed or things moving too quickly for her because as his hands slid between her thighs and met her heat she was moaning and he was pushing her onto the bed, with Jasmine wondering where her inhibitions had gone.

She had hundreds of them, Jasmine reminded herself as he knelt over her and examined every inch of her, his eyes greedy with want.

A telephone book full of them.

Or she had, but they had just all disappeared today.

It was almost impossible to tear the packet for him.

And she found herself licking her lips as he slid it on.

She had never had sex like it.

She had never felt less mechanical in her life.

Thought had been replaced by pure sensation.

Him, she thought as he got back to kissing her.

Her, he thought as he reclaimed her mouth.

And then the power that remained sort of fused into one.

His fingers were there and she was wet and warm and wanted this just as much as he did.

'First time since…' She sort of braced herself and he held back and took a moment to not be selfish, even if she wanted him to be. Instead, he slid deeper into her with fingers that were skilled and frantic, and she left it to him, because he knew what he was doing. If they were quick it was mutual, if they were fast it was with begging consent.

Even with much preparation she was incredibly tense when the moment came and she willed him to ignore her. Slowly he pushed in, and she stretched and resisted and then stretched again, and he gave her a moment of stillness to get used to him inside.

Well, not really a moment because he knew he only had a few left in him but Jed left it for her to initiate movement, felt the squeeze and the pull on him as she tested herself as she moved herself up and down his long length.

Just when she thought she had adjusted, just when she pulled him in, he beat her to it and drove into her, and she met him and then he did it again and she tried to trip into his rhythm, except he was so hard and fast now it was bliss to not try, to simply let him, only it wasn't a passive response, it was more trusting.

Jed could hear Jasmine's moans and her urging, and he wished for a second she'd be quiet, because it made it impossible for Jed not to come, except she was starting to. He felt the lift of her hips and the arch of her into him, the feel of a slow uncurling from the inside, reluctant almost to give in to him, and then as he moaned his release she shattered.

She did, she just gave in in a way she never had, felt and delivered deeper than she ever had, and found out in that moment how much of herself she had always held back, the intensity fusing them for a moment in absolute bliss.

She lay there trying to get her breath back as he rested on top of her, and still they were one as reality slowly started to intrude.

She wasn't ready for a relationship.

He'd sworn to not get involved with someone from work.

Penny.

Promotion.

Simon.

Single mum.

Simultaneously the real world flooded its lights onto them and they both turned looked at each other for a long moment.

'Well,' Jasmine said. 'We must have both needed that.'

He laughed, actually laughed on the inside too as he had when she had mouthed 'sorry', and the doubts that had started hushed.

And they hushed some more as they lay in bed and drank Vanessa's sparkling wine that hadn't even had time to cool, and they congratulated each other on how fantastic that had been, rather than trying to work out where they were, and then she told him not what was on her mind but the truth.

'I have to go to sleep.'

'And me.'

'I hardly slept yesterday.'

'Me neither.'

'Jed, I don't know what happened. I don't really know what to say.' She was as honest as she could be. 'I'm nowhere near ready to get involved with someone, so I don't really know how we ended up here.'

'I do,' Jed admitted. 'Why the hell do you think I've been avoiding you since I found out you weren't married?'

'What?'

He just shrugged.

'Tell me.'

'You just…' He gave an embarrassed grin. 'Well, you know when you're attracted to someone? I suppose when I saw you talking to Penny and then she said you were here for an interview and then someone called you Mrs Phillips, well, I was relieved you were spoken for.'

Jasmine frowned.

'I don't like mixing work with things and thought I might have trouble keeping to that with you—it wasn't a logical thing, just…'

She did know what he meant.

Maybe it hadn't been quite an instant attraction, but that evening on the beach, when he'd lifted his T-shirt… Jasmine pulled back the sheet, looked at his lovely abdomen and bent over and ran her fingers lightly over the line there. He caught her hand as it moved down.

'I thought you wanted to sleep.'

'I do.'

'Then later.'

She set the alarm for that afternoon, before she remembered another potential problem. Penny.

'And no one at work is to know.'

'Suits me.'

'I mean it,' Jasmine said. 'What happened yesterday at work was wrong.'

'I'll carry on being horrible.'

'Good.'

'So much for clearing the air,' Jed said. 'Now it's all the more complicated.'

'Not really,' Jasmine yawned. 'Just sleep with me often and buy me lots of chocolate. My needs are simple.'

For that morning at least it really did seem as straightforward as that.

CHAPTER NINE

JED WAS NICE and grumpy at work and he deliberately didn't look up when she walked past, and Jasmine made sure there were no private jokes or smiles.

Gossip was rife in this place and the last thing she wanted was to be at the centre of it again.

No one could have guessed that their days were spent in bed. She just hoped he understood that it couldn't always be like this—that night shifts and her mother's help had made things far easier than they would be from now on. In fact, Jed got his first proper taste of dating a single mum that weekend.

Ruby was lovely.

'I'm hoping to work overseas as a nanny,' she explained to Jasmine, 'so I'm trying to get as much experience as I can and hopefully by the time I've got my qualification I'll have a couple of good references.'

She was very good with Simon, happy to sit with him as he tried to bang square pegs into round holes, and Jasmine could tell Ruby was very used to dealing with young children.

'My main problem is late shifts,' Jasmine explained.

'The crèche knows me,' Ruby said. 'I pick Liam up and I take him back to Vanessa's. I give him his dinner and bath and I try to get him asleep for Vanessa but Liam likes to wait up for her.'

Jasmine laughed. She and Vanessa had got the boys together a couple of times and Liam certainly had plenty of energy.

'Well, Vanessa and I aren't working the same shifts so much now,' Jasmine explained, 'so if we can try and work opposite late shifts…'

'It will all work out,' Ruby said. 'I can always look after them both some evenings.'

Jasmine was starting to think this could work.

So much so that for a try-out Ruby suggested she look after Simon that night, and for the first time in a very long time Jasmine found herself with a Saturday night free. To her delight, when Jed rang a little bit later she found that she had someone to share it with.

'It went well with Ruby, then?'

He asked about the babysitter as they were seated for dinner.

'She seems lovely,' Jasmine said. 'Simon didn't even get upset when I left.'

They were eating a couple of suburbs away from the Peninsula Hospital in a smart restaurant that overlooked the bay. Jasmine had taken a taxi because she hadn't been out in yonks and she wanted a glass or three of wine.

'I would have picked you up.'

'I know.' Jasmine smiled. 'But I've a feeling Ruby might gossip to Vanessa. I feel like I'm having an affair. It's too confusing to work out…' She looked up from the menu and went cross-eyed and Jed started to laugh.

'I can't do that.'

'It's easy,' Jasmine said. 'You just look at the tip of your nose and then hold it as you look up.'

'You've practised.'

'Of course.' She grinned.

And, cross-eyed or not, she looked stunning, Jed noted.

Her hair was loose as it had been on the day he had met her on her walk on the beach, but it fell in thick glossy curls. Unlike at work, she was wearing make-up, not a lot but just enough to accentuate her very blue eyes and full mouth. 'What do you want to eat?'

'Anything,' Jasmine said. 'Well, anything apart from chicken nuggets.'

So instead of leftover nuggets there was wine and seafood, and conversation was easy, as long as it was just about food, about movies and the beach, but the second it strayed deeper there was a mutual pulling back.

'Will you go back to your maiden name?' Jed asked after a while.

'I don't know,' she admitted. 'I don't know if I should change Simon's…'

'So what is it?'

'Sorry?'

'Your maiden name?'

She didn't answer him, just peeled a prawn. She didn't even get a reprieve when he asked what had happened in her marriage, because for a marriage to break up when someone was pregnant it sounded as if something pretty serious had.

'I've got three hours, Jed.' She smiled, dipping a prawn in lime mayonnaise. 'In fact, two hours and fifteen minutes now. I want to enjoy them, not spend time talking about my ex.'

And later, when they were finishing up their heavenly dessert and he mentioned something about a restaurant in Sydney, she asked why he'd moved. His answer was equally vague and Jasmine frowned when he used her line.

'We've got thirty minutes till you need to be back for Ruby. Do we really want to waste them hearing my woes?'

'No.' She laughed.

But, yes, her heart said, except that wasn't what they were about—they had both decided.

They were going to keep things simple and take things slowly.

But it was difficult to find someone so easy to talk to and not open up, especially when the conversation strayed at one point a little too close to Penny. She'd mentioned something about how good it was to have Ruby, given her mum and sister were so busy with their jobs. As soon as she said it she could have cut out her tongue.

'Your mum's in real estate?' Jed checked, and she nodded. 'What does your sister do?'

It was a natural question but one she'd dreaded.

'She does extremely well at whatever she puts her mind to,' Jasmine evaded, reaching for her glass of wine.

'Ouch.' Jed grinned. 'Sore point?'

'Very.'

So he avoided it.

It was nice and going nowhere, they both knew that. It was an out-of-hours fling, except with each turn it became more complicated because outside work there were Simon and Penny and unbeknown fully to the other the two hearts that were meeting had both been incredibly hurt.

Two hearts that had firmly decided to go it alone for now.

They just hadn't factored in desire.

'It's like being a teenager again.' Jasmine grinned as he pulled the car over before they turned into her street and kissed her. 'My mum lives in this street.'

'We're not outside…?'

'No.'

'Good,' he said, and got back to kissing her.

They were under a huge gum tree that dropped gum nuts everywhere, but Jed risked the paintwork, grateful for the leafy shield, and they were ten minutes into a kiss that was way better than teenage ones she'd partaken in, right on this very spot, especially when Jed moved a lever and her seat went back a delicious fraction.

She could hardly breathe. He was over her and looking down at her, his hand was creeping up between her legs, and she could feel how hard he was. However, they could not take it even a fraction further here and she was desperate to pay Ruby and have her out of there, wanted so badly to have him in her bed.

And it would seem that Jed was thinking the same thing. 'I could wait till Ruby's gone.'

'No.' She hauled the word out, for if she regretted using it now, she knew she would regret it more in the morning if she didn't. 'I don't want that for Simon.' She looked up at those gorgeous eyes and that mouth still wet from her kisses and it killed her to be twenty-six and for it to feel wrong to ask him in. 'We're keeping things light,' Jasmine said. 'Agreed?' she prompted, and he nodded. 'Which is fine for me, but I won't treat his little heart lightly.'

'I know.'

'Next time we'll go to yours,' Jasmine suggested.

He looked down at her and the rules he'd embedded into his brain were starting to fade, because he had enjoyed being out, but now he wanted in.

'We'll see,' he said, because this was starting to be about a whole lot more than sex. He'd more than enjoyed tonight, had loved being in her company. The only bit that was proving difficult was leaving things here. 'Maybe we'll go out but eat more quickly?'

'Confusing, isn't it?' she said, and again she crossed her eyes and he laughed and then one more kiss and it ached to a halt.

Killed to turn on the engine and drive down the street and then turn into her own street and to park two doors down from her home.

To smile and walk out and to rearrange her dress as she let herself in.

To chat and pay Ruby and carry on a normal conversation, saying that, yes, she'd had a great night catching up with an old friend, and maybe she'd ask Ruby to babysit so that they could catch up again, perhaps as soon as next week.

But a week didn't seem so soon once Ruby was gone.

A night felt too long.

It killed her not to text him to come back.

CHAPTER TEN

'HI, JASMINE!'

She looked up at the familiar face of a paramedic who was wheeling a stretcher in.

'I haven't seen you in ages.'

'Hi, Mark.' Jasmine smiled, but there was a dull blush on her cheeks, and as Jed looked over to see how the new patient was, he couldn't help but notice it, couldn't help but see that Jasmine was more than a little flustered as she took the handover. 'What are you doing out here?'

'We're all over the place today,' Mark said. 'I had a transfer from Rosebud that got cancelled and then we were called out to Annie here.' Jasmine smiled at her new patient. 'Annie Clayfield, eighty-two years old, fell at home last night. We were alerted by her security when she didn't respond to their daily phone call. We found her on the floor,' Mark explained. 'Conscious, in pain with shortening and rotation to the left leg.'

He pulled back the blanket and Jasmine looked at the patient's feet and saw the familiar deformity that was an obvious sign of a hip fracture.

Annie was a lovely lady and tough too—she tried to hold back her yelp of pain as they moved her over as gently as they could onto the trolley.

Jed came over when he heard her cry and ordered some analgesic.

'We'll get on top of your pain,' Jed said, 'before we move you too much.' He had a listen to her chest and checked her pulse and was writing up an X-ray order when he saw one of the paramedics leave the stretcher he was sorting out and head over to Jasmine.

'So you're here now?'

'That's right.' Jed noted that her voice was falsely cheerful and he had no reason to listen, no reason not to carry on and see the next patient, except he found himself writing a lot more slowly, found himself wanting to know perhaps more than he should if they were planning to keep things light.

'I heard you and Lloyd split up?'

'We did.'

'What's he doing with himself these days?'

'I've no idea,' Jasmine said. 'We're divorced now. I think he's working in his family's business.'

As Jed went to clip the X-ray slip to Annie's door he saw the paramedic give Jasmine a brief cuddle.

'You had nothing to do with it, Jasmine, we all know that. You don't have to hide.'

'I'm not hiding.'

And there was no such thing as uncomplicated, Jed decided, looking at Annie's X-rays a good hour later and ringing down for the orthopaedic surgeons. They'd both agreed to keep it light, to take things slowly. Neither of them talked much, about families or friends or the past, and it should suit him, and yet the more he knew, or rather the less he got to know...

The more he wanted.

Despite all efforts to take things slowly, things were

gathering pace between them. They'd been seeing each other for a few weeks now—at least, whenever they got a chance.

They rang each other a lot, and went out whenever shifts and babysitters permitted, or more often than not they ended up back at his for a few stolen hours.

It just wasn't enough, though.

Concentrate on work, he told himself as he ran along the beach that night.

Except she was home, he knew it.

And Simon would be in bed.

And she wanted to keep that part of her life very separate.

So too did he, Jed reminded himself.

He caught sight of the city shimmering gold in the distance. Melbourne offered a gorgeous skyline but a different skyline from the one he knew so well.

He'd come here to get away, Jed reminded himself.

To finally focus on his career and get ahead.

Yet he looked at the tall gleaming buildings of Melbourne and as much as he loved Peninsula, there was something about the city, or rather a busy city emergency department.

And still Melbourne Central beckoned.

CHAPTER ELEVEN

JASMINE STARED AT the roster and gritted her teeth.

Jed was filling out blood forms and suitably ignoring her, and Penny was at her annoying best, suggesting that the nurses join her in Resus so that she could run through a new piece of equipment with them.

A new piece of equipment that had been there as long as Jasmine had and had been used often.

Honestly, the second the place was finally quiet Penny found a job or an activity for everyone.

No wonder she was so unpopular.

The roster had finally been revealed for the next eight-week period and as she tapped the shifts into her phone Jasmine could feel her blood pressure rising.

Yes, she was the new girl.

Yes, that meant that she got the rubbish shifts—but she had more late duties coming up than she could count, and lots of weekends too, which she would usually be glad of for the money, but of course the crèche wasn't open on weekends and, even though she'd been told it was only about once every three months, there was *another* stint of nights coming up in two weeks.

Her mum would be on her cruise by then.

'Problem?' Lisa checked.

'Just the nights,' Jasmine said. 'I thought it was every three months.'

'Well, we try and share it, but especially when someone's new I like to get them to do some early, so that was an extra for you.'

Was she supposed to say thanks?

She liked Lisa, Jasmine really did, and she was running a department after all, not Jasmine's childcare arrangements, but the pressure of shift work and single parenting, let alone trying to date, was starting to prove impossible.

Idly flicking through the patient bulletin, her eye fell on the perfect job for a single mum who actually wanted to have a little bit of a life too.

It was in the fracture clinic and was almost nine to five.

It was a level above what she was on now, but with her emergency experience she would stand a pretty good chance at getting it.

'Fracture Clinic!' Vanessa peered over her shoulder. 'You'd go out of your mind.'

'I'm going out of my mind looking at the roster,' Jasmine admitted.

'Don't think about it,' Vanessa said breezily. 'Something always turns up.'

Jasmine rolled her eyes as Vanessa walked out. 'I wish I had her optimism.'

'Jasmine.' She turned and smiled at the sound of Mark's voice. 'How are things?'

'Good.' Jed saw she was uncomfortable, saw she glanced over her shoulder to check whether or not he was there, and it was none of his business, he wanted it that way, yet he wanted to know what the problem was, why Mark thought she was hiding.

'Just giving you the heads up, no doubt you'll be alerted soon, but there's a nasty car versus bike on the beach road. Sounds grim.'

'Do we know how many?' Jed asked.

'That's all I've got but they're calling for backup.'

'Thanks.'

Jasmine let Lisa know and the orthopods were down anyway, looking at a fractured femur, and Lisa said to just wait till they heard more before they started paging anyone but that she'd let Penny and Mr Dean know.

Then Mark's radio started crackling and he listened, translating the coded talk of the operator. 'They're just about to let you know,' Mark said. 'One fatality, one trapped, one on the way—adult male.'

The alert phone went then and Lisa took it just as Penny appeared, looking brusquely efficient as usual.

'Car versus motorbike,' Lisa said. 'We've got the biker coming in, he's conscious, abdominal injuries, hypotensive.' She looked up at the clock. 'He's five minutes away and they've just freed the trapped driver, so he's on his way too.'

'I'll take the first,' Penny said. 'If that's okay with you, Jed?'

'Be my guest,' Jed answered, but Jasmine saw the clenching of his jaw and knew that Penny was seriously rattling him—she was always jumping in, always trying to take over anything that was remotely interesting.

'Have we paged the surgeons?' Penny asked.

'Done,' Jasmine said.

'Blood bank?'

'I've let them know.'

Penny gave no response, but with reason as the blast of a siren told them the ambulance was here. As the paramedics raced the patient in, Jasmine didn't blame Penny a bit for the curse she let out when she asked where the hell the surgeons were.

The patient, though conscious, was beyond pale. His pulse was thin and thready and Jasmine set to work, with Greg cutting his leathers off.

'Can you tell me your name?' Penny asked as she examined him.

'Reece.'

'And do you know where you are?'

He answered the questions when prompted but kept closing his eyes and drifting off. Jasmine could only just palpate his blood pressure manually and Penny wasted no time in drawing blood for an urgent cross-match and telling the porters to run it up.

'And I mean run!' he warned. 'Let's put the O-neg up.'

Penny was possibly up there with the most horrible doctors Jasmine had worked with. She was abrupt to the point of rudeness, gave no thanks, only barked demands, except…

She was brilliant.

'If they can't be bothered to get down here,' Penny shouted as Jasmine tried to locate the surgeons again, 'tell them that I'll meet them up in Theatre.'

The patient had had a spinal and chest X-ray, and despite the O-negative blood being squeezed in, his blood pressure was still barely discernible. It was clear he needed Theatre and Penny wanted him taken straight up.

Jed was dealing with the latest admission, and Jasmine quickly prepared Reece for theatre, loading his clothes into a bag and itemising his valuables—rings, wallet… But as she opened up the wallet Jasmine hesitated. There were loads of hundred-dollar notes—at best guess the wallet contained a few thousand dollars.

'Can someone check this with me?' Jasmine asked.

'I'll check it with you later,' Greg called. 'Just put it in the safe.'

'Can we just check it now?' Jasmine pushed, except Greg wasn't listening, so she popped her head around the curtain to where Vanessa and Lisa were assisting Jed. 'Can someone check this, please? He's got a large amount of cash.'

'Just pop it in the safe,' Lisa called. 'I'll count it when things have calmed down.'

'We're supposed to check it before we put it in the safe.' Jasmine's voice was shrill. 'We're not supposed to sign—'

'Here.' It was Penny who stepped in. 'Give it to me, Nurse. I'll put it in the safe.' She walked over and took the wallet, signed the piece of paper and threw the contents into the safe. Jasmine realised that she was sweating and she could feel Jed's eyes on her.

'Right,' Penny said. 'We need to get him up or he's going to bleed out.' She picked up the phone and told Theatre the same as Jasmine prepared the trolley for an emergency transfer, but her hands were shaking and her heart was thumping as she knew she'd made a bit of a scene.

'All okay, Jasmine?' Lisa checked as Jasmine walked past to get a space blanket to put over Reece on the way up to Theatre.

'We're just about to move him,' Jasmine said, and as Jed briefly looked up she felt the question in his brief gaze, knew she wasn't fooling anyone that everything was okay, least of all Jed.

'Reece.' Jasmine tried to explain things as best she could as she covered him with the space blanket. He was irritable now and struggling to remain conscious, and he wanted to wait till his wife got there before he went up. 'We're going to have to move you to Theatre now. Miss Masters will explain things.'

Which Penny did.

She was efficient, brusque but also terribly kind. 'I know you want to wait for your wife—I completely understand, but you're too sick,' she explained gently but firmly. 'I will talk to your wife myself as soon as she gets here. Is there anything you want me to say to her?' She glanced at Jasmine and Greg and at the anaesthetist who had just arrived. 'Could you all excuse us a moment?'

As Jasmine stepped outside to give Penny and Reece some privacy, there was a strange sting of tears in her eyes. It wasn't that she had seen a different side to her sister, rather she had seen a side to Penny that she had long forgotten.

Sitting on the stairs, hearing her parents argue, had terrified four-year-old Jasmine. It had been Penny who would take her back to bed, Penny who would sit beside her and tell her not to worry, that she would take care of things, that even if things did get bad, that even if Dad did what he was threatening and left, they would be fine.

'But what if we're not?' Jasmine would argue. 'What if we never see him?'

'Then we'll deal with it.'

And in their own ways and albeit not perfectly they had.

And as she ran up to Theatre with her sister, and

Penny told her to head back down, that she wanted to speak with surgeons, Jasmine knew that she hadn't just come back for the support of her family, neither had she taken the job here for the reasons she had so determinedly given.

She wanted to be close to Penny again.

CHAPTER TWELVE

'I'LL COME OVER after work.'

Jed was coming out of X-Ray as Jasmine walked back from Theatre and they found themselves walking together towards Emergency.

'It's fine.' Jasmine shook her head. 'I'll see you at the weekend. Ruby said that she could—'

'But you're upset tonight.'

'Don't worry, I'll be fine by Saturday.' She couldn't keep the brittle edge from her voice. Yes, she was happy keeping things light, but sometimes, on days like today, it was hard.

'I'm not expecting to be entertained,' Jed said. 'What happened back there?'

'Nothing.'

'Jasmine? Why did you get all upset over the safe? You know we can't just drop everything—the guy was bleeding out.'

'Just leave it.'

But Jed wouldn't.

It was a very long shift. Vanessa was on a half-day and Jasmine really wished that she herself was—she could feel Jed watching her, especially much later when Lisa came over and asked her to check the cash.

'Four thousand six hundred dollars. Agreed?' Lisa checked.

'Agreed,' Jasmine said, and because Penny had first signed for it, she had to be there too.

'I just rang ICU,' Penny said. 'He's doing much better. His wife told me that he was on his way to put down a deposit on a car—that's why he had so much cash on him.' She added her signature to the valuables book.

'Oh, the irony of it,' Lisa sighed, because in a car his injuries would have been so much less. 'Now, I know this is a lot of money and that it has to be checked,' Lisa continued, 'but it's not always possible to just drop everything. It's better to put it in the safe.'

'That's not what the protocol says,' Jasmine pointed out, and Lisa pursed her lips. 'It's been six hours now.'

'I didn't know you were such a stickler for protocol and guidelines, Nurse,' Penny smirked. 'The irony of it!'

'What was that about?' Lisa grinned when Penny waltzed off.

'I think that might have been Penny's attempt at humour,' Jed said, but she could feel his eyes on her, knew he was trying to talk to her, but as she had all day she did her best to avoid him.

Jasmine actually thought she had when she finally finished for the day and went to pick Simon up. But heading over to the crèche she found Jed at the vending machine outside.

'I'll come over later.'

'You know I don't want that. I don't want to confuse Simon.'

'We're not going to make out on the sofa,' Jed said. 'And I'm not going to stay the night till you think he's ready for that, but I do want to talk to you. You're nearly in tears and I don't get why. What happened at your old job?' He could see the blush on her cheeks but she said nothing, instead walked past him to pick up Simon.

Simon was happy and scruffy after a day in the sand-pit and Jasmine knew that it was time to face things, that she and Jed could not keep skirting around the edges.

Here in her hands was the living proof of an exceptionally difficult relationship, here was the baggage she carried, and yet it felt right in her arms.

She had to be able to talk about it with someone she trusted.

And she had to start trusting Jed.

He was still waiting for her when she headed outside.

'About six?'

'He'll still be up.'

'I don't mind, or I can come over around nine if that's what you'd prefer?' She longed to let Jed closer but she just couldn't take any chances with Simon.

'About nine.'

Simon wasn't at his sunniest and her mum dropped over too. It was just one of those disorganised evenings, not helped by a disorganised brain thanks to the day's events. Jasmine had just got Simon down and was sorting out his bag for the next day when she heard a knock at the door and looked up to see that it was already a quarter past nine.

'I wouldn't have got here at six anyway,' Jed said, following her through to the kitchen. 'I only just got away. It's still busy there.'

'Who's on?'

'Rex!' Jed rolled his eyes. 'And Penny's still hovering. I swear she never sleeps.'

'Do you want something to eat?'

'Are you going to cook for me?' Jed grinned.

'No,' Jasmine said, 'but if you're nice I might defrost something.'

Actually, she did cook. Well, she made some pasta and defrosted some sauce and it was possibly their most normal night together. He ate a large bowl while Jasmine got things ready for the next day. Perhaps realising she wasn't ready to talk yet, he chatted a bit more about himself, telling her a bit about his siblings and their families.

'Don't you miss them?'

'A lot.'

'So how come you moved down here?'

'Just…' Jed shrugged. He knew he had to tell her, but there would be time for all that later—he wasn't here for himself tonight. He could see that she was still upset, see her hands shake a little as she folded some washing and then finally joined him.

'You got upset in Resus today.'

'I didn't.'

'Jasmine?'

'I just get annoyed when people don't check valuables properly,' she attempted. 'Everyone bangs on about how important it is and then if something goes missing…'

'People are busy.'

'I know that.'

'I heard you speaking to that paramedic,' Jed admitted, and he watched as she closed her eyes. 'Jasmine, did something happen at your old job?'

'No,' she broke in. 'Jed, please…' And then she started to cry. 'I found out that my husband was stealing from patients.' It was so awful to say it, to admit to it. She'd made it so huge in her mind that she half expected him to stand up and walk out, but of course he didn't. Instead, he took both her hands.

'Come on.' He was very kind and very firm but he wasn't going to leave it. 'Tell me what happened.'

'I don't know where to start,' she said. 'There was an unconscious patient apparently and there was a lot of money missing.' She knew she wasn't making much sense, so she just told him everything.

'Lloyd,' Jasmine said. 'Simon's father, he was a paramedic. We really got on, but then everyone did with Lloyd. He was very popular. We went out for about three months and—' she couldn't really look at that time properly '—I thought everything was fantastic at first,' she admitted. 'But I know now that it wasn't because I was being lied to even then. I didn't know but there had been a report put in about him.'

'You can't know if someone doesn't tell you,' Jed pointed out.

'I know that, but it wasn't just that he didn't tell me.' She took a deep breath, because if she was going to tell him some of it, then she had better tell him all. 'Remember I told you that I can't take the Pill?' She blushed as she had the first time she'd told him. 'Well, we were careless.' She went really red then, not with embarrassment, more with anger. 'Actually, no, we weren't. I know it takes two, but I think he was the one who was careless.'

'Jasmine.' Jed was completely honest. 'I nearly forgot our first time.'

'I know,' she admitted. 'But even if you had, I've got a coil now, so it wouldn't matter. It was more that I didn't forget.' She looked at Jed, she knew how they had lost it in bed together, but she never had till him. 'I reminded him, I tried to stop him. I don't know, I can't prove that, but there was an accident, and I found I was pregnant and not sure I wanted to be. I was just so confused and yet he was delighted. He insisted we get married and and then we took three months off to see Australia. As he said, to have loads of fun before the baby. I had lots of annual leave saved up.'

She couldn't even look at Jed as she went on. 'What Lloyd hadn't told me was that he was under investigation for stealing from a patient. It was all kept confidential so not even his colleagues knew, but another patient had come forward with a complaint and they'd placed Lloyd on three months' paid suspension. We were swanning around Australia and I had no idea.'

'When did he tell you?'

'He didn't,' Jasmine admitted. 'I went back to work. I was coming up for six months pregnant by then and he told me that he had another month off and then he started to talk about how, given I love my work, why didn't we think about him staying home to look after the baby? Every word that man said to me was a lie.' She could feel her anger rising as it did whenever she thought about him and wondered, as she often did, if he'd got her pregnant deliberately.

'So how did you find out?'

'The other paramedics were a bit cool with me,' Jasmine admitted. 'They're a pretty honourable lot, they don't take kindly to what Lloyd did and there was I, chatting with them like I used to, about our holiday, about things, and then one of my friends pulled me aside and said it might be better if I didn't rub things in.' She started to cry. 'She said it was fine if I could accept what he'd done, but it was a bit much for them to hear about us having fun with his suspension pay. He'd been fired by then and I didn't even know.'

'Oh, Jasmine.'

'He said that as his wife I should have supported him, but the fact is I wouldn't have married him had I known.' She looked at Jed. 'I wouldn't have. I'm not saying someone has to be perfect, I'm not saying you don't stick together through bad times, but I didn't even know that he was in the middle of bad times when we got married, when he made sure I was pregnant.' She was really crying now. 'I moved out and kept working right till the end of my pregnancy, but it was awful. I think my friends believed I had nothing to do with it, that I hadn't had a clue…'

'Of course they did.'

'No.' Jasmine shook her head. 'Not all of them—there was loads of gossip. It was just awful at the time.

'I see some of the paramedics now and we're starting to be friendly again,' she continued. 'I think they really do understand now that I simply didn't know. I'm just trying to get on with my life.'

'Do you speak to him at all?'

'Nothing,' Jasmine said. 'He came and saw Simon a couple of times when we were in the hospital, but there's been nothing since then. He's got a new girlfriend and so much for being a stay-home dad—he doesn't even have a thing to do with his son. He's working in the family business, they're all supporting him, as families do, and making sure it looks like he earns a dollar a week, so I don't get anything.'

'You can fight that.'

'I could, but I don't want to,' Jasmine said. 'I don't want any of his grubby money. I stayed close by for a year because, at the end of the day, I figured that he is Simon's dad and I should make it as easy for him as possible to have access to his son. But when he wanted nothing to do with him…' She was a little more honest than she'd expected to be. 'I was embarrassed to go back to work too. He just completely upended my life.'

And Jed got that, he got that so much, how one person could just walk into your life and shatter it, could make a normal world suddenly crazy, and he could have told her then, but Jed knew that now wasn't the time.

'And I'm the one left holding the baby.' She was the most honest she had been with another person. 'And I know if it hadn't happened then I wouldn't have Simon and I love him more than anything so I can't wish it had never happened, except sometimes I do.'

Of course she heard Simon crying then, just to ram home the guilt of her words.

'I need to go and settle him.'

'Sure.'

Simon didn't want settling, Simon wanted a drink and a play and a conversation.

'He's not going to settle.' She came back into the living room a good twenty minutes later.

'Do you want me to leave?'

'No,' Jasmine said. 'But I'm going to have to bring him in here.'

'Are you sure?' Jed checked.

'It's no big deal,' Jasmine said.

Except they both knew that it was. Jed hadn't seen Simon since that day on the beach when he'd helped get him into the water.

And Jed really didn't want to leave her.

Simon was delighted with the late night visitor, chatting away to him for as long as he could till his eyes were heavy and Jasmine put him back to bed.

'Cute,' Jed said. 'He looks like you—apart from the blond hair. Is his dad blond?'

'No,' Jasmine replied. Simon was a mini, male Penny.

'Have you told Lisa what happened?'

Jasmine shook her head.

'I think you might feel better if you did.' He was very practical. 'You did nothing wrong, but you know what rumours are like and it might be better to just tell Lisa up front what happened,' Jed said. 'And then you can stop worrying about it. If anyone does bring it up, Lisa will just blow them off.

'And…' he gave her a smile '…she might be a bit more understanding when patients land in the department with their life savings stuffed in a carrier bag.'

'I think I might,' Jasmine said. 'Thanks.' It was actually nice to have told someone and telling Lisa was a good idea.

'I'd better go,' Jed said. 'It's one thing having a friend over, but different me still being here in the morning. What are you on tomorrow?'

'I'm on a late,' Jasmine said. 'Ruby's picking Simon up from crèche.'

'How's that working out?'

'Good,' Jasmine admitted. 'She's really sensible and he seems to adore her. Simon's usually in bed by about seven so she gets her homework done.

'Stay if you like,' Jasmine said, 'I mean…'

'I know what you mean.' And he looked over at Jasmine and for the first time things were starting to get serious, and he didn't feel hemmed in. In fact, he wanted more of this and was sure that Jasmine was someone he could open up to about his past. She just didn't need it tonight. 'Are you sure?' Jed checked. 'He might wake up again.'

'He might.' Jasmine looked up at him. 'Look…' She didn't really know how to say it without sounding needy, but she had Simon to think of so she had to be brave. 'I want to see more of you, Jed.' His eyes never left her face. 'I'm the same as you. I don't want this to carry over to work, which means that if we are going to see more of each other… I'm not asking for for ever, but if you're thinking this isn't working out then say so now.'

'I think it is working out.'

'And I'd like to see you a bit more than a couple of hours once a week.'

'Me, too.'

'Stay, then,' she said.

It was all a bit different having Simon in the house with them.

Like at midnight when they were kissing on the sofa, instead of things leading to wherever they might lead, she had to check on Simon, who was whimpering with his teeth. By the time she'd given him some medicine and rubbed some gel on his gums, Jed was sitting up in her bed, reading his horoscope in one of her trashy magazines.

Except he put it down as she started undressing.

'Don't,' Jasmine said, because he had an unfair advantage, well, two actually. He was already in bed and also with a body like his there was no need to be embarrassed about stripping off in front of another person.

'Why are you shy now?'

'I don't know.' She actually wasn't shy, she felt guilty for what she had said. 'Thanks,' she said as she slipped into bed. 'For hearing me out and what I said about wishing it had never happened.'

'I'd be the same,' Jed said, shuddering at the thought of how much worse things might have been for him—and he closed his eyes for a moment, imagining the last couple of years with a baby added to the mix. And he turned and he almost told her, but he could see her eyes were still swollen from crying and it simply wouldn't be fair to her.

'Imagine if he hadn't stolen the money,' Jed said. 'You could have spent your life married to a guy who was crap in bed.'

He saw the start of a smile.

'Go on,' he said. 'Say it.'

'No.' Jasmine kicked him. 'Anyway, you don't know that he was.'

'Please.' Jed rolled his eyes.

'So much for not getting involved with anyone from work.' He looked down at her before he kissed her. 'I think we should keep it separate, though,' Jed said. 'I really mean that.'

She was incredibly glad to hear it. 'I'm the same.'

'Things are a bit sensitive at the moment,' he said.

'With the promotion?' It was an entirely innocent question, or at least she'd thought it was, but Jed stopped kissing her and frowned.

'You've heard about that?'

'Sorry.' She tried to play for time.

'How did you hear about that?'

She was glad for the lights being off for another reason now. Her face was on fire in the dark from her slip-up.

'I don't know,' she attempted. 'You know what that place is like, there's always talk.'

'I guess.' He let out a long sigh. 'Oh, well, if it's out there's nothing I can do about it. At least I know no one heard it from me.'

He forgot about it then but it took a while for Jasmine to.

He kissed her till she almost had, she kissed him back till she nearly did, but it was there at the back of her mind, just how complicated things were and he didn't even know.

'Are you all right?' He lifted his head.

'Just tense.'

She almost told him, she nearly did.

Except she'd promised her sister that she wouldn't.

'I can fix that.'

And he slid beneath the sheets and she lay there biting her lip, thrashing with her thoughts as his tongue urged her to give in.

He was incredibly patient.

Didn't seem to mind a jot how long it took.

And she tried to relax to the probe of his tongue. To forget her problems, forget Penny and Lloyd and everything really except...

'Jed?'

He didn't answer.

'Jed?' She had to tell him, had to tell him now. 'Things are complicated.'

'Not from where I am,' Jed said, lifting his head just a little. 'You worry too much.'

Maybe she did, Jasmine realised, closing her eyes to the mastery of his mouth.

He gave her no room to think about it anyway. His

hands lifted her buttocks so he could concentrate his efforts and he homed in, she pushed on his shoulders, because she should surely tell him, except he pushed back on the pressure she exerted and obliterated her thoughts with his tongue.

He was determined now, felt the shift in her, and it turned him on further. He loved feeling her unbend beneath him, loved the constant fight with her busy mind, and he would win this one and he felt her quiver as he worked on her most tender spot.

He felt her thighs start to tighten and the moans in her throat and he loved the wrestle within in her, loved how her hands moved from his shoulders and to his head, how her body begged him to continue while her mouth urged him to stop.

And then she gave in to him, shocked that he didn't stop there, that when he should surely abate he worked harder, and she throbbed into him and still his mouth cursed her restraint. Still his tongue told her there was more, and there was.

He rose over her in the dark, his hand moved to the bedside and it was hers that stopped him, stopped a man who, very kindly, never forgot.

'I told you,' she said. 'I've got the coil.'

And he smiled down at her as just once she said it. 'And, yes, as I've since found out—he was crap in bed.'

There was nothing to complicate or confuse right now, just the bliss of him sliding inside her, and for Jed he had never been closer to another, just lost himself in her. It was more than sex and they both knew it—it was the most intimate either had ever been. He thrust into her as he wanted to and she tightened her legs around him. He could hear the purr in her throat and feel the scratch of her nails on his back and she knew that, however they denied it, this was fast becoming serious.

And yet there were secrets between them.

For Jed there were no secrets, or there soon wouldn't be. He'd already made the decision to tell her, he just had to find the right time and tonight wasn't it. He felt her tighten around him, loved the intimacy and feeling her without the barrier of a sheath, loved the sob into his shoulder and the sudden demand within her that gave Jed permission to let go, which he did, but not fully. He lifted up on his arms and felt every beat of pleasure that shot out of him, he felt every flicker of hers, except he held back on the words that seemed most fitting right now.

He lay there afterwards and he should have been glad he hadn't said them. Neither of them were ready for love, but for Jed it was starting to feel like it.

And for Jasmine too, she felt as if they were on the edge of something, something that neither had seen, a place they had never intended to go. Except he was in bed beside her and it felt as if he should be, and she knew what to do now.

She wasn't waiting for the interviews, and Penny would just have to deal with it if it confused things.

Tomorrow, or at the very next opportunity, she would tell Penny.

Then she could be completely honest with Jed.

Then, Jasmine decided, there would be no holding back.

CHAPTER THIRTEEN

JED WAS GONE before Simon woke up, but her resolve was the same and once she'd given Simon his breakfast and got him dressed, Jasmine picked up the phone and rang Penny.

'What are you doing, ringing me at work?' Penny sounded irritated at the intrusion.

'It's the only chance I get to speak to you,' Jasmine said. 'Of course I can talk to you there if you prefer.'

'No, this is fine,' Penny sighed. 'What did you want?'

'I was hoping we could catch up away from work. There's something I'd like to talk about, something I need to check with you.'

'Fine,' Penny said.

'Tonight?' Jasmine asked.

'I'm going out tonight.' And she was working the next one. 'I'm going to Mum's on Sunday for dinner—how about then?'

Jasmine really didn't want to discuss this in front of their mother, but maybe they could go for a walk afterwards, or she could suggest that Penny go back to her place for a coffee?

'Sounds good.'

'So, when are you working again?' Penny asked.

'In a couple of hours' time.' Jasmine smiled. 'I promise to keep on ignoring you.'

As she dropped Simon off at crèche, Jasmine realised that things were starting to work out—she was starting to think that this was maybe doable and that nine-to-five job in the fracture clinic might not be necessary after all. Vanessa's mum was looking after Liam this evening, which meant that Ruby would pick Simon up from crèche and take him back to Jasmine's. Her baby-sitting arrangements were all under control, if a touch too expensive, but it was worth it to be doing a job she loved and for the first time since way before Simon's birth things were starting to look stable.

Well, not stable. Her heart leapt in her throat still at the sight of Jed and she was shaky with all the rush of a new romance, but the rest of her life seemed to be slotting together when just a few weeks ago it had seemed an impossible dream.

There was actually no chance to speak to Lisa about anything personal, or Jed, come to that. The department was incredibly busy and the late shift flew by, so much so that Jasmine blinked in surprise when Lisa caught her on the way up to the ward with a geriatric patient and lightly scolded her for not taking her breaks.

'I had no idea of the time,' Jasmine admitted, surprised to see it was already seven o'clock. 'I'll just take this one up to the ward.'

'Well, make sure that when you get back you take a break,' Lisa said. 'I don't care how busy the place is, I don't want my staff burning out.'

Lisa was always insistent that her staff take their allotted breaks, and often she would ring Admin and have a nurse sent down from the wards during particularly busy periods.

After handing her patient over, Jasmine realised she was actually hungry and stopped at the vending machine for chocolate to take to her break. 'It's crazy out there,' Vanessa greeted her when she got back to the staffroom. 'Did Lisa tell you off for not taking a break?'

'She did,' Jasmine said, slipping off her shoes. 'Maybe it's going to be a full moon tonight. I don't envy the night staff.'

'It will be your turn again soon.'

'I know,' Jasmine groaned.

'Did you speak to Ruby about staying over while you're on nights?'

'I did,' Jasmine said. 'She can do the first week. The problem is with the weekend on the second.'

'I can help you with that,' Vanessa said. 'If you can help out next month when it's my turn?' She gave Jasmine a nice smile. 'It all works out in the end.'

'I know,' Jasmine admitted. 'I think I've got to stop looking too far ahead and take things more day by day.'

'That's all you can do when you've got little ones.'

Right now, Jasmine was looking forward to it being nine o'clock so that she could go home. Jed got off duty at ten and had promised to bring food, which meant she had just enough time to chat with Ruby and then hopefully have a quick shower before Jed arrived.

Yes, she was starting to think that things might work out.

'Are you going to that?' Vanessa broke into her thoughts.

'Sorry?'

'It's the accident and emergency ball in a couple of weeks.' Vanessa pointed to the rather impressive poster

up on the staff noticeboard. 'It's the big fundraiser for
the department. Apparently there are still some spare
tickets.'

Jasmine's eyes widened when she saw the price of
the tickets and she wasn't surprised that there were still
a few left.

'I doubt I'll be going.' Jasmine shook her head as she
broke off some chocolate. Especially when she factored
in the price of the new dress, hair, shoes and paying a
babysitter. 'Are we expected to go?'

'Not really,' Vanessa said. 'It's really more for the
bigwigs. Mind you, it will be a fun night—there's always loads of gossip whizzing around after an emergency do—we can have our fun with that afterwards,
even if we can't be there.' Vanessa gave a mischievous
smile. 'Still, it's a shame that we won't get to watch Jed
and Penny studiously avoiding each other and trying to
pretend that they're not together.'

Jasmine felt her blood run cold. She couldn't quite
believe what she was hearing. 'Jed and Penny?'

'Didn't you know?' Vanessa was idly watching the
television as she spoke and didn't see Jasmine's appalled
expression and carried on chatting, blissfully unaware
of the impact of her words. 'They've been on and off
since Jed started here, not that they would ever admit
to it, of course. Heaven forbid that Penny brings her
personal life into work and be so reckless as to display
human tendencies.' Vanessa's words dripped sarcasm.
'God knows what he sees in her.'

'Maybe he doesn't.' Jasmine was having great trouble
speaking, let alone sounding normal. 'Maybe he doesn't
see anything in her. It's probably just gossip—you know
what this place can be like.'

'I wish,' Vanessa sighed. 'Jed is just gorgeous. He's wasted on that cold fish. But I'm afraid that this time the hospital grapevine is right—Greg walked in on them once and you can hardly miss the tension between them.' She turned and looked at Jasmine. 'I can't believe you haven't noticed. It's an open secret, everyone knows.' Vanessa stood up. 'Come on, we'd better get back out there.'

Except Jasmine couldn't move.

'I'll be along in a moment,' Jasmine said. 'I shan't be long.'

Her hand was clenched around the chocolate so tightly it had all melted, not that she noticed till Vanessa had gone and Jasmine stood up. She headed for the bathrooms—she didn't just feel sick, she actually thought she might vomit as she washed the mess off her hands. She held onto the sink and tried to drag in air and calm her racing thoughts before heading back out there.

Not once had it entered her head that Penny and Jed might be together.

Not one single time.

And Penny had never so much as hinted that she was seeing someone.

But, then, why would she?

Penny never told Jasmine what was going on in her life. Her engagement had ended and Penny had said nothing about it other than it was over. She certainly never invited discussion. Jasmine, in turn, had never confided in Penny. Even when her marriage had been on the rocks, Jasmine had dealt with it herself—telling her mum and Penny that it was over only when her decision had already been made.

She should have listened to Penny, Jasmine realised.

She should never have worked in the same department as her sister.

Jasmine scooped water from the sink into her hand and drank it, tried to calm herself down. Somehow she had to get through the rest of her shift.

Jed was coming round tonight.

Jasmine spun in panic at the thought.

She would talk to him... And say what?

If there was anything between him and Penny she would just end it and move to the fracture clinic.

Or back to Melbourne Central, because that sounded quite a good option right now. And if that sounded a lot like running away from her problems, well, at that moment Jasmine truly didn't care. As much as she and Penny didn't get on very well, never in a million years would she do that her sister.

Except it would seem that she already had.

'You seem in a hurry to escape the place,' Penny commented.

'For once, yes,' Jed said. 'It's all yours.'

He had more on his mind tonight than a busy department.

Tonight he was going to tell Jasmine the truth about what had happened with Samantha.

It was an unfamiliar route Jed was considering taking and one he was not entirely comfortable with. He was way too used to keeping things in. He'd avoided anything serious since his last break-up. Sure, he'd had the occasional date, but as soon as it had started to be anything more than that, Jed had found himself backing away. And as if to prove him right, the texts and tears that had invariably followed had only strengthened his resolve not to get attached and to step away. Except for the first time he felt as if he could trust another person. After all, Jasmine had opened up to him.

Jed wasn't stepping away now.

Instead, he was stepping forward.

He rang ahead to his favourite restaurant and ordered a meal for two, but despite confidence in his decision there was more than a touch of nerves as he paid for his takeaway and headed back to the car, as he built himself up to do what he said had sworn he would never do— share what had happened, not just with someone he was starting to get close to…but with someone he was starting to get close to from work.

'Hi.'

Jasmine opened the door and let him in, still unsure what she should say, how best to broach it. Did she really want to know that he was with her sister? Did she really want Jed to find out the truth?

Surely it would better to end it neatly?

To get out before they got in too deep?

Except she was in too deep already.

'I bought Italian,' Jed said, moving in for a kiss, 'but to tell the truth I'm not actually that hungry.'

She'd meant to carry on normally, to sit down and discuss things like adults while they were eating, but as he moved in to kiss her, just the thought that he might have been with Penny had Jasmine move her head away.

'Jasmine?' She saw him frown, heard the question in his voice about her less-than-effusive greeting, but she didn't know how to answer him. Despite three hours trying to work out what she might say to him, how best to approach this, she still didn't know how and in the end settled for the first thing that came into her head.

'I'm not sure that you ought to be here.'

'Sorry?'

'I don't think this is working, Jed.'

'It would seem not.'

Of all the things he had been expecting tonight, this wasn't one of them. Sideswiped, Jed walked through to the lounge and put the takeaway down on her coffee table, completely taken aback by the change in Jasmine. They'd made love that morning, he'd left her smiling and happy, with no hint of what was to come. 'Can I ask what has changed between this morning and tonight?'

'I just think things have moved too fast.'

'And could you not have decided this before you introduced me to Simon?' He didn't get it and he knew she was lying when he saw her blush. 'What's going on, Jasmine?'

'I heard something at work today,' Jasmine admitted. 'Something about you.'

'So it's gospel, then?' was Jed's sarcastic response. 'And while you were listening to this gossip, did you not consider running it by me first, before deciding we that weren't working?'

'Of course I did,' Jasmine attempted. 'That's what I'm doing now.'

'Is it even worth asking?' Jed said. 'Because it sounds to me as if the jury is already in. So, what is it that I'm supposed to have done?'

'I heard…' Jasmine swallowed because it sounded so pathetic, especially with how good he had been with her secret last night, but still she had to find out for sure. 'I heard that you and Penny…'

'Penny?'

'Someone told me that you and Penny…' She couldn't

even bring herself to say it, but the implication was clear and Jed stood there and shook his head.

'Jasmine, we agreed from the start that as erratic as things may be for us you and I wouldn't see anybody else so, no, I'm not seeing Penny.'

'But have you?' Jasmine asked. 'Have you dated Penny in the past?'

'What on earth…?' He just looked at her, looked at her as if he'd suddenly put glasses on and was seeing her for the first time and not particularly liking the view. 'I'm being dumped because the hospital grapevine states that I might be or in the past might have slept with a colleague?' He shook his head. 'I never took you for the jealous kind, Jasmine.'

'I just need to know.'

But Jed wasn't about to explain himself. 'Look, I don't need this.' He didn't confirm it and he didn't deny it and she honestly didn't know what to do. She could feel tears pouring down her cheek.

'Jed, please,' she said. 'Just tell me. I need to know if there's ever been anything between you and Penny.' She was starting to cry and she knew she had to tell him, no matter how awkward it made things for them, no matter the hurt to Penny, she just had to come right out and say it, and she was about to, except Jed didn't give her a chance.

'You want a complete itinerary of my past?' Jed said. 'What do you want, a full list of anyone I've ever dated so you can check them out online?'

'Jed, please,' Jasmine attempted, but he wasn't listening to her now.

'You're the one with the past, Jasmine. You're the one who's just had her divorce certificate stamped and has a baby sleeping in the bedroom and an ex who stole from patients. Did I ask for a written statement, did I ask for facts and details?' He turned to go and then changed his mind, but he didn't walk back to her. He picked up his takeaway and took it. 'I'm hungry all of a sudden.'

He headed out to his car and drove off, but only as far as the next street, and it was there that Jed pulled over and buried his head in his hands.

He couldn't believe it.

Could not believe the change in her—the second they'd started to get serious, the moment he'd actually thought this might work, he'd been greeted with a list of questions and accusations and for Jed it all felt terribly familiar.

After all, he'd been through it before.

CHAPTER FOURTEEN

THE WEEK HAD been awful.

Jed was back to being aloof, not just with her but with everyone, and on the occasions they had to work together he said as little as he could to her.

And now, when she'd rather be anywhere else, she sat at her mother's, eating Sunday lunch with Penny and wondering how on earth she could ever tell her and if it would simply be better if Penny never found out.

Which sounded to Jasmine an awful lot like lying.

'You wanted to talk to me.'

'I just wanted a chat,' Jasmine said. 'We haven't caught up lately.'

'Well, there's not really much to catch up on,' Penny said. 'It's just work, work, work.'

'It's your interview soon,' Louise reminded her.

'You haven't mentioned it to anyone?' Penny frowned at Jasmine. 'I told you about that in confidence. I shouldn't have said anything.'

'I haven't,' Jasmine said, but her face burnt as she lied.

'Well, I've heard that there are rumours going around, and if I find out that it's you...' Penny gave a tight shrug. 'Sorry, that was uncalled for. I just hate how gossip spreads in that place.'

'Are you going to the A and E ball?' Jasmine tried to change the subject, attempting to find out what she simply had to know.

Not that it would change anything between her and Jed.

Not just because of the possibility that he and Penny had once been an item, more the way he had been when they'd had a row. He hadn't given her a chance to explain, had just thrown everything she had confided to him back in her face and then walked out.

She didn't need someone like that in her life and certainly not in Simon's—still, she did want to know if the rumours were true, which was why she pushed on with Penny, dancing around the subject of the A and E ball in the hope it might lead to something more revealing.

'I've been asked to put in an appearance,' Penny said, helping herself to another piece of lamb. 'Why?' she asked. 'Are you thinking of going?'

'Not at that price,' Jasmine said. 'I just wondered if you were, that's all.'

'I have to, really. Jed and I will probably take it in turns—someone has to hold the fort and all the consultants will want to be there.'

'Jed?' Louise asked.

'The other senior reg,' Penny explained.

'The one who's going for the same position?' Louise checked, and Penny gave a curt nod.

'You and Jed...' The lovely moist lamb was like burnt toast in Jasmine's mouth and she swallowed it down with a long drink of water. 'Are you two...?' Her voice trailed off as Penny frowned.

'What?'

She should just ask her really, Jasmine reasoned. It

was her sister after all—any normal sisters would have this conversation.

Except they weren't like normal sisters.

Still, Jasmine pushed on.

She simply had to know.

'Is there anything between you and Jed?'

'If you're hoping for some gossip, you won't get it from me. I don't feed the grapevine,' Penny said, mopping the last of her gravy from her plate. 'So, what did you want to talk about?'

And really the answer didn't matter.

She and Jed were over. If he had slept with Penny she just wanted to be as far away from them both as possible when the truth came out. 'I'm thinking of taking the job in the fracture clinic.'

Penny looked up.

'Why?'

'Because…' Jasmine shrugged '…it's not working, is it?'

'Actually, I thought it was,' Penny said. 'I was worried at first, thought you'd be rushing to my defence every five minutes or calling me out, but apart from that morning with the baby…' She thought for a moment before she spoke. 'Well, seeing you work, you'd have said the same to any doctor.' She gave her sister a brief smile. 'You don't have to leave on my account. So long as you can keep your mouth shut.'

Her mum had made trifle—a vast mango one with piles of cream—and normally Jasmine would have dived into it, but she'd lost her appetite of late and Penny ate like a bird at the best of times. Louise took one spoonful and then changed her mind.

'I must have eaten too fast,' Louise said. 'I've got terrible indigestion.'

'I'll put it back in the fridge,' Jasmine said, clearing the table.

'Take some home,' her mum suggested. 'I don't fancy it.' She smiled to Simon, who was the only one tucking in. 'He can have some for breakfast.'

'Jasmine.' Penny caught her as she was heading out of the front door. 'Look, I know I kicked up when I found out you were going to be working in Emergency.' Penny actually went a bit pink. 'I think that I went a bit far. I just didn't think we could keep things separate, but things seem to be working out fine.'

'What if you get the consultant's position?' Jasmine checked. 'Wouldn't that just make things more difficult?'

'Maybe,' Penny said. 'But I don't think it's fair that you have to change your career just because of me. You're good at what you do.'

It was the closest she had ever come to a compliment from her sister.

'Look,' Penny said, 'I do want to talk to you if that's okay—not here…not yet.' She closed her eyes. 'It's…' She blew out a breath. 'Look, you know how I bang on about work and keeping things separate? Well, maybe I've being a bit of a hypocrite.'

'Are you seeing someone?'

'It's a bit more complicated than that.' Penny shook her head. 'Let me just get the interview over with. I mustn't lose focus now.' She let out a wry laugh. 'Who knows, I might not even get the job and then there won't be a problem.'

'Sorry?' Jasmine didn't get it. 'I thought you were desperate to be a consultant.'

'Yes, well, maybe someone else might want the role more than I do,' Penny said. 'Forget I said anything. We'll catch up soon.'

And as Jasmine lay in bed that night, she was quite sure she knew what the problem was.

Penny was worried that if she got the position it might hurt Jed.

For the first time in a long time Penny was actually putting another person before herself. She actually cared about another person.

The same person her younger sister had been sleeping with.

Monday morning was busy—it always was, with patients left over from a busy weekend still waiting for beds to clear on the ward, and all the patients who had left things till the weekend had passed seemed to arrive on Emergency's doorstep all the worse for the wait. Jed didn't arrive in the department till eleven and was wearing a suit that was, for once, not crumpled. He was very clean-shaven and she knew he wasn't making any effort on her behalf, especially when Penny came back from a meeting in Admin and her always immaculately turned-out sister was looking just that touch more so.

Clearly it was interview day.

She had to leave.

It really was a no-brainer—she could hardly even bear to look at Penny. She made the mistake of telling Vanessa on their coffee break that she was going to apply for the fracture clinic job.

'You'd be bored senseless in the fracture clinic.' Vanessa laughed as they shifted trolleys to try to make space for a new patient that was being brought over. Unfortunately, though, Vanessa said it at a time when Lisa and Jed were moving a two-year-old who had had a febrile convulsion from a cubicle into Resus.

'I'd be glad of the peace,' Jasmine said, and she would be, she told herself, because she couldn't go on like this. It wasn't about the workload, more about having to face Jed and Penny every day and waiting for the bomb to drop when he found out that she and Penny were sisters.

She could not face her sister if she ever found out that she and Jed had been together, even if it had been over for ages.

But then she looked over and saw that Lisa and Jed were there and, more, that they must have heard her talking about the fracture clinic job.

She wasn't so much worried about Jed's reaction— no doubt he was privately relieved—but Lisa gave her a less-than-impressed look and inwardly Jasmine kicked herself.

'Sorry,' Vanessa winced. 'Me and my mouth.'

'It's my fault for saying anything,' Jasmine said, but there wasn't time to worry about it now. Instead, she took over from Lisa.

'Aiden Wilkins. His temp is forty point two,' Lisa said. 'He had a seizure while Jed was examining him. He's never had one before. He's already had rectal paracetamol.'

'Thanks.'

'He's seizing again.' Just as Lisa got to the Resus door, Aidan started to have another convulsion. Jed gave him some diazepam and told Jasmine to ring the paediatrician, which she did, but as she came off the phone

Jed gave another order. 'Fast-page him now, also the anaesthetist.'

'Everything okay?' Penny stopped at the foot of the bed as Vanessa took the mum away because she was growing increasingly upset, understandably so.

'Prolonged seizure,' Jed said. 'He's just stopped, but I've just noticed a petechial rash on his abdomen.' Penny looked closely as Jed bought her up to speed. 'That wasn't there fifteen minutes ago when I first examined him.'

'Okay, let's get some penicillin into him,' Penny said, but Jed shook his head.

'I want to do a spinal. Jasmine, can you hold him?'

Speed really was of the essence. Aiden needed the antibiotics, but Jed needed to get some cultures so that the lab would be able to work out the best drugs to give the toddler in the coming days. Thankfully he was used to doing the delicate procedure and in no time had three vials of spinal fluid. Worryingly, Jed noted it was cloudy.

Jasmine wheeled over the crash trolley and started to pull up the drugs when, as so often happened in Resus, Penny was called away as the paramedics sped another patient in.

'Penny!' came Lisa's calm but urgent voice. 'Can I have a hand now, please?'

'Go,' Jed said. 'I've got this.'

The place just exploded then. The paediatrician and anaesthetist arrived just as an emergency page for a cardiac arrest for the new patient was put out.

'Jed!' Penny's voice was shrill from behind the curtain. 'Can I have a hand here?'

'I'm kind of busy now, Penny.' Jed stated the obvious and Lisa dashed out, seeing that Jed was working on the small toddler and picked up the phone. 'I'm fast-paging Mr Dean...' She called out to the anaesthetist, whose pager was trilling. 'We need you over here.'

'Call the second on.' Jed was very calm. 'He's stopped seizing, but I want him here just in case.'

'You call the second on,' Lisa uncharacteristically snapped and looked over at the anaesthetist. 'We need you in here now.'

It was incredibly busy. Jed took bloods and every cubicle in Resus seemed to be calling for a porter to rush bloods and gasses up to the lab. Jed was speaking with the paediatrician about transferring Aiden to the children's hospital and calling for the helicopter when Lisa came in to check things were okay.

'We're going to transfer him,' Jasmine explained.

'I'll sort that,' Lisa said. 'Jasmine, can you go on your break?'

'I'm fine,' Jasmine said. After all, the place was steaming.

'I don't want the breaks left till midday this time. Let's get the breaks started. I'm sending in Greg to take over from you.'

Jasmine loathed being stuck in the staffroom when she knew how busy things were out there, but Lisa was a stickler for breaks and really did look after her staff. That didn't stop her feeling guilty about sitting down and having a coffee when she knew the bedlam that was going on.

'There you are.' Lisa popped her head in at the same time her pager went off. 'I just need to answer this and then, Jasmine, I need a word with you—can you go into my office?'

Oh, God.

Jasmine felt sick. Lisa must have heard her say she was thinking of handing her notice in. She should never have said anything to Vanessa; she should have at least spoken to Lisa first.

Pouring her coffee down the sink, Jasmine was torn.

She didn't want to leave, except she felt she had to, and, she told herself, it would be easier all round, but she loved working in Emergency.

Would Lisa want a decision this morning? Surely this could wait.

She turned into the offices, ready for a brusque lecture or even a telling-off, ready for anything, except what she saw.

The registrar's office door was open and there was Penny.

Or rather there was Penny, with Jed's arms around her, oblivious that they had been seen.

He was holding her so tenderly, his arms wrapped tightly around her, both unaware that Jasmine was standing there. Blinded with tears, she headed for Lisa's office.

Her mind made up.

She had to leave.

CHAPTER FIFTEEN

'I'M SORRY!' LISA walked in just as Jasmine was blowing her nose and doing her best to stave off tears. 'I really tried to speak to you first before you found out.'

So Lisa knew too?

'How are you feeling?' Lisa asked gently. 'I know it's a huge shock, but things are a lot more stable now...' She paused as Jasmine frowned.

'Stable?'

'Critical, but stable,' Lisa said, and Jasmine felt her stomach turn, started to realise that she and Lisa were having two entirely separate conversations.

'I've no idea what you're talking about,' Jasmine admitted. 'Lisa, what am I here for?

'You don't know?' Lisa checked. 'You seemed upset... just then, when I came in.'

'Because...' Because I just saw my sister in Jed's arms, Jasmine thought, and then she wasn't thinking anymore, she was panicking, this horrible internal panic that was building as she realised that something was terribly wrong, that maybe what she had seen with Penny and Jed hadn't been a passionate clinch after all. 'What's going on, Lisa?' Jasmine stood up, more in panic, ready to rush to the door.

'Sit down, Jasmine.' Lisa was firm.

'Is it Simon?' Her mind raced to the childcare centre. Had something happened and she hadn't been informed? Was he out there now, being worked on?

'Simon's fine,' Lisa said, and without stopping for breath, realising the panic that not knowing the situation was causing, she told Jasmine, 'Your mum's been brought into the department.'

Jasmine shook her head.

'She's very sick, Jasmine, but at the moment she's stable. She was brought in in full cardiac arrest.'

'When?' She stood to rush out there.

'Just hold on a minute, Jasmine. You need to be calm before you speak to your mum. We're stabilising her, but she needs to go up to the cath lab urgently and will most likely need a stent or bypass.'

'When?' Jasmine couldn't take it in. She'd only been gone twenty minutes, and then she remembered the patient being whizzed in, Lisa taking over and calling Mr Dean, Penny calling for Jed's assistance.

'Penny?' Her mind flew to her sister. 'Did Penny see her when she came in?'

'She had to work on your mum.' Lisa explained what had happened as gently as she could. 'Jed was caught up with the meningococcal child and I didn't want you finding out that way either—unfortunately, I needed you to be working.'

Jasmine nodded. That much she understood. The last thing she would have needed at that critical time in Resus was a doctor and a nurse breaking down before help had been summoned.

'And Penny told me to get you out of the way.' Jasmine looked up. 'She told me you were her younger sister and that you were not to find out the same way she had… She was amazing,' Lisa said. 'Once she got over the initial shock, she just…' Lisa gave a wide-eyed look of admiration. 'She worked on your mother the same way she would any patient—she gave her the very best of care. Your mum was in VF and she was defibrillated twice. By the time Mr Dean took over, your mum was back with us.'

'Oh, God,' Jasmine moaned and this time when she stood, nothing would have stopped her. It wasn't to her mother she raced but to next door, where Penny sat slumped in a chair. Jed was holding a drink of water for her. And to think she'd begrudged her sister that embrace. No wonder Jed had been holding her, and Jasmine rushed to do the same.

'I'm so sorry, Penny.'

She cuddled her sister, who just sat there, clearly still in shock. 'It must have been a nightmare.'

Penny nodded. 'I didn't want you to see her like that.'

She had always been in awe of Penny, always felt slightly less, but she looked at her sister through different eyes, saw the brave, strong woman she was, who had shielded the more sensitive one from their parents' rows, had always told her things would be okay.

That she'd deal with it.

And she had. Again.

'It's my fault,' Penny grimaced. 'Yesterday she was ever so quiet and she said she had indigestion. It must have been chest pain.'

'Penny.' Jasmine had been thinking the same, but hearing her sister say it made her realise there and then what a pointless route that was. 'I had indigestion yesterday. We all did. You know what Mum's Sunday dinners are like.'

'I know.'

Jasmine looked up at Jed. His face was pale and he gave her a very thin smile. 'I'm sorry to hear about your mum,' he said, and then he looked from Jasmine to Penny and then back again. 'I had no idea.'

'Well, how could you have?' Penny said, and then turned to Jasmine. 'Can you go and see Mum? I can't face it just yet, but one of us should be there.'

'Of course.'

'She'll be scared,' Penny warned. 'Not that she'll show it.'

'Come on,' Jed said. 'I'll take you round to her.'

Once they walked out of the door he asked what he had to. 'Jasmine, why didn't you say?'

'She'd made me promise not to.'

'But even so…'

'I can't think about that now, Jed.'

'Come on.' He put his arm round her and led her into her mum's room, and even if it was what he would do with any colleague, even if she no longer wanted him, she was glad to have him there strong and firm beside her as she saw her mum, the strongest, most independent person she knew, with possibly the exception of her elder sister, strapped to machines and looking very small and fragile under a white sheet.

'Hey, Mum.'

Jasmine took her hand.

'I'm sorry,' Louise said, but for once her voice was very weak and thin.

'It's hardly your fault. Don't be daft.'

'No.' She was impatient, despite the morphine, desperate to get everything in order before she went to surgery. 'I haven't been much support.'

'Mum!' Jasmine shook her head. 'You've been wonderful.'

'No.' She could see tears in her mum's eyes. 'Most grandmothers drop everything to help with their grandchildren.'

'Mum,' Jasmine interrupted. 'You can stop right there. I'm glad you're not like most mums, I'm glad Penny is the way that she is, because otherwise I'd be living at home even now. I'd be dumping everything onto you and not sorting my own stuff out, which I have,' Jasmine said firmly, and then wavered. 'Well, almost.' She smiled at her mum. 'And that's thanks to you. I don't want a mum who fixes everything. I want a mum who helps me fix myself.'

'Can I see Simon?' She felt her mum squeeze her hand. 'Or will I scare him?'

'I'll go now and get him.' Before she left, Jasmine looked at Jed.

'I'll stay.'

And it meant a lot that he was with her.

Oh, she knew Mr Dean was around and Vanessa was watching her mother like a hawk, but it wasn't just for medical reasons it helped to have Jed there.

She couldn't think of that now.

The childcare staff were wonderful when Jasmine told them what was going on. 'Bring him back when you're ready.'

'Thanks.'

Jasmine really didn't know if it would terrify Simon or how he'd react when he saw his nanny, but she knew that the calmer she was the better it would be for Simon.

'Nanny's tired,' Jasmine said as they walked back to the department. 'She's having a rest, so we'll go and give her a kiss.'

He seemed delighted at the prospect.

Especially when he saw Penny standing at the bed. Then he turned and saw Jed there and a smile lit up his face.

'Jed!'

He said it so clearly, there was absolutely no mistake, and Penny's eyes were wide for a second as she looked at Jed, who stood, and then back at Penny.

'I'll have to put in a complaint,' Penny said. 'The hospital grapevine is getting terribly slack.'

'Tell me about it,' Jed said, but whatever was going on, whatever questions needed answers, it was all put aside as Simon gave his nanny a kiss and a cuddle. He was amazing, not bothered at all by the tubes and machines, more fascinated by them, if anything, pointing to the cardiac monitor and turning as every drip bleeped. But of course after a few moments he grew restless.

'We're going to take your mum up to the catheter lab soon,' Vanessa said. The cardiac surgeon had spoken to them in more detail and her mum had signed the consent form, and it was all too quick and too soon. Jasmine had just got used to the idea that she was terribly ill and now there was surgery to face.

'Can I just take Simon back?'

'Of course.' And in the few weeks she'd been here, Jasmine found out just how many friends she had made, just how well she was actually doing, thanks to her mum. 'Tell the crèche that I'll pick up Simon tonight. He can stay at my place.'

'You're sure?' Jasmine checked. 'I can ring Ruby.'

'It's fine tonight. You'll probably be needing Ruby a lot over the next few days. Let me help when I can.'

The crèche was marvellous too and told Jasmine that she could put Simon in full time for the next couple of weeks, and somehow, *somehow* Jasmine knew she was coping with a family emergency and single motherhood and work combined.

And she didn't want to lose her job, no matter how hard it would be, working alongside Jed.

Except she couldn't think about it now.

Right now, her heart was with her mum, who was being wheeled out of Emergency, a brusque and efficient Penny beside her, telling the porter to go ahead and hold the lifts, snapping at Vanessa for not securing the IV pole properly, barking at everyone and giving out orders as she did each and every day, while still managing to hold her mum's hand as she did so.

And her heart wasn't just with her mum.

It was with her big sister too.

The time sitting in the Theatre waiting room brought them possibly the closest they had ever been.

'Is that why you were asking about Jed and I?'

They were two hours into waiting for the surgery to finish, an hour of panic, ringing around friends and family, and then an hour of angst-filled silence, and then, because you could only sit on a knife edge for so long, because sometimes you needed distracting, Penny asked the question that was starting to filter into both their minds.

'For all the good it did me.' Jasmine smiled. 'How come we don't gossip?'

'I never gossip,' Penny said. 'I don't do the girly thing and...' Her voice trailed off and she thought for a moment, realising perhaps how impossible for her sister this had been. 'You could have asked me, Jasmine.'

'What if I didn't like the answer?' Jasmine's eyes filled with tears and she couldn't start crying again. She'd shed more tears since her mother had gone to Theatre than she had in a long time.

'You're still not asking me.'

Jasmine shook her head, because if the truth were known she was scared to. Not just for what it would do to her but what the truth might mean for her sister.

'Nothing has ever happened between Jed and I.'

Jasmine felt as if a chest drain had been inserted, or what she imagined it must feel like, because it felt as if for the first time in days, for the first time since Vanessa had inadvertently dropped the bomb, her lungs expanded fully, the shallow breaths of guilt and fear replaced by a deep breath in.

'Nothing,' Penny said. 'Not a single kiss, I promise you.' And Jasmine could now breathe out. 'Who said that there was something going on between us?'

'It's common knowledge apparently, though I only heard this week. My friend couldn't believe that I hadn't notice the tension between you two.'

'The only tension between us,' Penny continued, 'is who might get the promotion.'

'I thought you were worried about getting it and upsetting Jed.'

Penny just laughed. 'Worrying about upsetting or upstaging Jed Devlin is the furthest thing from my mind— believe me. Do I look like someone who would step aside from a promotion for a man?' She actually laughed at the very thought.

'No,' Jasmine admitted. 'But you did say you weren't sure if you wanted the job…'

'Right now I'm not even thinking about work, I just want Mum to get well, that's as far as I can think today. You have nothing to worry about with Jed and I.'

'It doesn't matter.'

'It clearly did.'

But Jasmine shook her head. 'I'm just glad I haven't hurt you—Jed and I are finished.'

'Jasmine!'

But Jasmine was through worrying about Jed. She didn't have the head space to even think about him right now. 'Let's just worry about Mum for now, huh?'

'How is she?' Lisa asked when an extremely weary Jasmine made her way down to Emergency the next morning.

'She's had a really good night,' Jasmine said. 'They're going to get her out of bed for a little while this morning, can you believe?'

'They don't waste any time these days.' Lisa smiled. 'How are you?'

'Tired,' Jasmine admitted. 'I'm sorry to mess you around with the roster.'

'Well, you can hardly help what happened. Have you got time to go through it now—did you want the rest of the week off?'

Jasmine shook her head. 'I was actually hoping to come in to work tomorrow—Penny's going to stay with her today and I'll come back this evening, but I'd rather start back at work as soon as possible. I might need some time off when she comes out, though.'

'We'll sort something out,' Lisa said. 'We're very

accommodating here, not like the fracture clinic.' Lisa winked.

'Sorry about that.'

'Don't worry about it for now. We'll have a chat when you're up to it.'

'Actually,' Jasmine said, 'do you have time for a chat now?'

She sat in Lisa's office and, because she'd got a lot of her crying out when she'd told Jed, Jasmine managed to tell Lisa what had happened with her ex-husband without too many tears, and was actually incredibly relieved when she had.

'You didn't need to tell me this,' Lisa said. 'But I'm very glad that you did. I'd rather hear it from you first and it's a good lesson to us all about being less careless with patients' property. I can see why you panicked now. Anyway...' she smiled, '...you can stop worrying about it now.'

Finally she could, and only then did Jasmine fully realise how much it had been eating at her, how much energy she had put towards worrying about it, running from it.

'Go home to bed,' Lisa said.

'I will. But I just need to have a quick word with Vanessa, if that's okay?'

Vanessa was one burning blush when they met. 'Simon's been fantastic. He's tucked up in the crèche now and I can have him again tonight if you like.'

'I'll be fine tonight.'

'Well, why don't I pick him when my shift's finished and bring him home to you?' Vanessa offered, and as Jasmine thanked her she suddenly cringed. 'Jasmine, I am so embarrassed.'

'Why?'

'All the terrible things I said about Penny. I could just die. I keep going over and over them and then I remember another awful thing I said.'

Jasmine laughed. 'Believe me, you weren't the only one, and you told me nothing about Penny that I didn't already know—Penny too, for that matter. It's fine, I promise.'

'Me and my mouth!' Vanessa grimaced.

'Forget it.' Jasmine smiled. 'Anyway, I'm going to go home to bed, and thank you so much for your help with Simon. I'm just going to pop in and give him a kiss.'

'Jasmine.' Just as he had on the first day they had met, Jed called her as she went to head out of the department. 'Can I have a word?'

'I'm really tired, Jed.'

'Five minutes.'

'Sure.'

'Somewhere private.'

They settled for one of the interview rooms.

'How is your mum?'

'Getting there.'

'How are you?'

'A lot better than yesterday,' Jasmine said. 'I'm really tired, though.'

'Of course.' He took a breath. 'You should have told me that you and Penny were sisters,' Jed said.

'You didn't exactly give me much chance.'

'Before that.'

'I was working up to it. But if we weren't serious there didn't seem any point.' She gave a tight shrug. 'I told you from the start I was trying to keep work and things separate—you were the same.' She turned to go. 'Anyway, it doesn't matter now.'

'We need to talk.'

'No,' Jasmine said. 'I don't think we do.'

'Nothing happened between Penny and I,' Jed said. 'Absolutely nothing. I can see now why you were upset, why you felt you couldn't ask.'

And now it was, Jasmine realised, time to face things properly, not make an excuse about being tired and scuttle off. 'It's actually not about whether or not you slept with Penny.' Jasmine swallowed. 'I mean, had you, of course it would have mattered.' He saw the hurt that burnt in her eyes as she looked up at him.

'You gave me no chance to explain,' Jasmine said. 'I was struggling—really struggling to tell you something, and you just talked over me, just decided I was too much hard work. You didn't even answer my question. You just threw everything back in my face.'

She would not cry, she would not. 'It took guts to leave my marriage,' Jasmine said. 'But it just took common sense to end things with you. In any relationship there are arguments, Jed.' She looked right at him as she said it. 'And from the little I've witnessed, you don't fight fair!'

She saw him open his mouth to argue, but got in first.

'That's a no in my book.'

CHAPTER SIXTEEN

HE RANG AND Jasmine didn't answer.

And she stayed at her mum's, ringing and answering the phone to various aunts and uncles so even if he went over to her place, she wouldn't know and more to the point she wasn't there.

'Cold tea bags help,' Penny said when she dropped around that evening and saw her puffy eyes. 'You don't want him to see that you've been crying.'

'I could be crying because Mum's in ICU.'

'She's been moved to Coronary Care,' Penny said, 'so you don't have that excuse.'

'They've moved her already?'

'Yes. Great, isn't it? And you've got the night off from visiting. She was sound asleep when I left her. Still, if you want to go in I can watch Simon.' She must have seen Jasmine's blink of surprise. 'I *am* capable.'

'I'm sure you are.' Jasmine grinned. 'I might just pop in, if you're sure.'

'Of course.'

'He's asleep,' Jasmine said. 'You won't have to do anything.'

'I'm sure I'll cope if he wakes,' Penny said. 'And if you are going to see Mum then you need to put on some make-up.'

It didn't help much, not that her mum would have noticed. She was, as Penny had said, asleep. Still, Jasmine felt better for seeing her, but that feeling faded about five minutes after visiting when she saw Jed coming out of X-Ray.

'Hi,' he said.

'Hi.'

'I tried to call,' Jed said, but Jasmine wasn't interested in talking.

'I need to get home.'

'Run off, then,' Jed said, and Jasmine halted for a second.

'Sorry?'

'You said you had to go.'

She opened her mouth to argue. Had he just accused her of running off? But instead of challenging him, she threw him a very disparaging look, and as she marched off, Jasmine knew she didn't need cold tea bags on her eyes—she was through crying.

Her mum was right—it was completely hereditary.

The Masters women had terrible taste in men!

Still, even if she would have liked to avoid him it was impossible at work. Everywhere she went she seemed to be landed with him, but she refused to let him get to her, refused to give him the satisfaction that she was running off.

But worse than the department being busy was the times it was quiet and though she had no idea who knew what, she nearly bit on her gums when Lisa gave her a very sweet smile.

'Could you give Jed a hand, please?' Lisa said, even

though there were five other nurses sitting around. 'He's stitching a hand and she won't stay still on the trolley.'

'Her name's Ethel,' Lisa added. 'You'll get to know her soon, she's one of our regulars.'

'Sure.'

She painted on a smile and walked into Theatre.

'Hi, there, Ethel, I'm Jasmine.'

'Who?'

She was an angry old thing, fuelled on sherry and conspiracy theories, and she made Jasmine laugh.

'Why would they knock the hospital down?' Jasmine asked patiently, when Ethel told her the plans were already in and had been approved by the council.

'Prime real estate,' Ethel said. 'Imagine how many townhouses they could put up here.'

'Have you been talking to my mum?' Jasmine grinned.

'All money, isn't it?' Ethel grumbled for a while and then spoke about her children, who, from the age of Ethel, must be in their sixties at least. 'They're just waiting for me to go,' Ethel said bitterly. 'Worried I'm spending their inheritance.' She peered at Jasmine. 'Have you got children?' she asked.

'None,' Jasmine happily lied.

'Husband?'

'Nope.'

'Good for you,' Ethel said. 'Dating?'

'Nope.'

'Quite right, too.' Ethel said. 'They're no good, the lot of them.' And she ranted for a few minutes about her late husband. 'They're all liars and cheats and if they're not now then they're just waiting to be. Nasty, the lot of them—except for the lovely doctor here.'

She caught Jed's eye and they actually managed a slightly wry smile.

'No, we're all horrible, Ethel,' Jed said. 'You're quite right not to listen to their sorry excuses.'

And if he'd looked up then he'd have seen Jasmine poke her tongue out.

'How's your mum?' Jed asked, when Ethel gave in and started snoring.

'Doing well,' Jasmine said. 'She should be home on Monday.'

'How are you?'

'Good,' Jasmine said, and hopped off the stool. 'It looks like she's sleeping. Just call out if you need a hand.'

'Sure,' Jed said, and carried on stitching as Jasmine went to wash her hands.

She knew he was just trying to irritate her as he started humming, knew he was just trying to prove he was completely unbothered working alongside her.

And then she realised what he was humming.

A little song that was familiar, a little song about a little runaway, and when he looked up at her furious face he had the audacity to laugh.

'You'd better go,' Jed said. 'It sounds busy out there.'

There were maybe five patients it the department.

'Or do you need to pop up to visit your mum?'

He teased her with every excuse she had ever made over the last couple of days whenever he had tried to talk to her.

'Or is it time to pick up Simon?'

And then he got back to humming his song.

'I'm not avoiding you or running away.'

'Good,' Jed said. 'Then I'll be over about eight.'

* * *

'I don't want to argue.'

As soon as she opened the door to him, Jasmine said it. 'I don't want raised voices…'

'I didn't come here for that,' Jed said. 'And I wouldn't do that to Simon and I certainly wouldn't do that to you.' He saw her frown of confusion as she let him in. 'You are right, though—I didn't fight fair.' He said it the moment he was inside. 'And I'm not proud of that. I didn't give you a chance to explain. I didn't give us a chance.'

He took a seat. 'And I get it that there were things that you couldn't talk about easily. I've thought about it a lot and I can see how impossible it was for you—after all, if you and Penny had agreed not to tell anyone…' He looked up at her. 'You could have told me—I would never have let on.'

'Perhaps not,' Jasmine said, 'but when I thought you two might have been seeing each other…' She looked at him. 'Penny insists nothing ever happened.'

'It didn't.'

'Apparently Greg walked in on you two once?' She wanted to believe her sister, but deep down she was still worried that it was Penny protecting her all over again.

'Greg walked in on us?' Jed gave a confused shake of his head, raked his fingers through his hair and pulled on it for a moment, then he gave a small smile as realisation hit. 'We had words once.'

'Words.'

'A lot of words. It was a couple of months ago,' Jed said, 'before you were around. In fact…' he frowned in recall, '…it was the same day as your interview. We had a busy afternoon and there was a multi-trauma that

I was dealing with and Penny just marched in and tried to take over.'

'I can imagine.' Jasmine gave a tight smile.

'And then she questioned an investigation I was running—Mr Dean was there and I think she was trying to…' he shrugged, '…score points, I guess. I don't do that.' Jasmine knew already that he didn't. 'And I don't mind being questioned if it's merited, but, as I told Penny, she's never to question me like that in front of a patient again or try and take over unless she thinks I'm putting a patient at risk.' Jed looked up at her. 'Which I certainly wasn't and I told her that.'

'Oh!'

'And I asked her to explain her thought process, her rationale behind questioning me,' Jed said. 'Which Penny didn't take to too well.'

'She wouldn't.'

'Your sister's lousy at confrontation, too.' Jed smiled.

'I don't think so.'

'Oh, she is,' Jed assured her. 'She only likes confrontation when it's on her terms. You should remember that next time she starts.'

And Jasmine found she was smiling.

'Greg walked in on us, actually, we were in the IV room, and, yes, I guess he picked up something was going on, but it certainly wasn't that.'

'So why wouldn't you answer me that day?' Jasmine asked. 'Why couldn't you just say that there was nothing going on between the two of you?'

'Because I've spent the last two years convincing myself I'd be mad to get involved with anyone at work.'

'Especially a single mum?'

'You could come with ten kids,' Jed said. 'It was never about that.'

'Then why?'

'Jasmine, please.' He put up his hand. 'This is difficult.' And she knew then he had something to tell her, that she was as guilty as he'd been that night, because she was the one now not letting him speak.

'I left my last job, not because...' He really was struggling with it. 'I got involved with a colleague,' Jed said. 'And there's no big deal about that, or there wasn't then. She worked in the labs in research and, honestly, for a couple of months it was great.' He blew out a breath. 'Then she started talking about children...'

Jasmine opened her mouth and then closed it.

'I wasn't sure. I mean, it was early days, but it wasn't even on the agenda. I told her that. She got upset and that weekend I went out with some friends. I was supposed to go over to hers on the Sunday and I didn't, no excuse, I just was out and got called into work and I forgot.' Jasmine nodded. She completely got it—she forgot things all the time.

'She went *crazy*,' Jed said. And it wasn't so much what he said but the way that he said it, his eyes imploring her to understand that this was no idle statement he was making. 'I got home that night and she was sitting outside my flat and she went berserk—she said that I was lying to her, that I'd met someone else.' He took a long breath.

'She hit me,' Jed said. 'But we're not talking a slap. She scratched my face, bit my hand.' He looked at Jasmine. 'I'm six-foot-two, she's shorter than you and there was nothing I could do. I could have hit her back, but I wouldn't do that, though, looking back, I think that was exactly what she wanted me to do.'

'Did you report it?'

He shook his head. 'What? Walk into a police station and say I'd been beaten up? It was a few scratches.'

'Jed?'

'I thought that was it. Obviously, I told her that we were done. She rang and said sorry, said that she'd just lost her head, but I told her it was over and for a little while it seemed that it was, but then she started following me.'

'Stalking?'

Jed nodded. 'One evening I was talking to a friend in the car park, nothing in it, just talking. The next day I caught up with her in the canteen and she'd had her car keyed—there were scratches all down the side. I can't say for sure that it was Samantha…'

'What did you do?'

'Nothing for a bit,' Jed said. 'Then my flat got broken into and then the phone calls started. It was hell.'

He had never been more honest, had been so matter-of-fact about it when he'd discussed it with others, but he wasn't feeling matter-of-fact now, because for the first time he was properly reliving that time. The flat tyres he'd come out to, the phone ringing in the night, that he didn't even want to think of dating, not because he didn't want to but because of what she might do to any woman he went out with.

'It all went from bad to worse. In the end she just unravelled—she ended up being admitted to Psych and nearly lost her job.'

'It's not your fault.' She saw the doubt in his expression. 'Jed, the same way I wasn't responsible for what my ex did.'

'That doesn't stop you looking back,' Jed said. 'I go over and over the time we were together and maybe I did let her think I was more serious than I felt.'

'Oh, come on, Jed. She clearly had issues. If it hadn't been you it would have been the next guy.'

'But it *was* me,' Jed said. 'I had more than a year of it. She's getting help now, apparently, but I just couldn't stay around,' Jed admitted. 'I don't think it was helping either of us to work in the same hospital and in the end I didn't want to even be in the same city. That's why I moved.'

'That's awful.'

'It was,' Jed said. 'I wasn't scared for myself, I could stop her physically, but when she started messing with people I knew, that was enough. And,' Jed added, 'I was scared for her too. It was awful to see someone who was basically nice just going to pieces.' He managed his first smile since he'd arrived that evening. 'Do you believe me now when I say I had no intention of getting involved with anyone at work?'

'Yes.'

'And do you understand why, when you got so upset that I might have once dated Penny, I thought it was all just happening again? I mean, the second we got serious, and we did get serious, you know that we did...' He waited till she nodded. 'Well, the next night I come round and you're standing there, crying and begging to know if I've ever hooked up with Penny, if anything, *anything* had ever happened between us.'

'I get it.' Jasmine even managed to laugh. 'I'd have freaked too, if I were you.' She went over to him and he pulled her onto his knee. 'I promise not to stalk you when we break up.'

'Maybe we won't.'

'We'll see,' Jasmine said.

'I know that you wouldn't now, anyway. You handled the break-up brilliantly,' Jed added. 'I mean, a couple of late night phone calls wouldn't have gone amiss—a few tears…'

Jasmine held her finger and thumb together. 'Just a smidge of obsession?'

'Careful what you wish for, huh?' Jed smiled back. 'I think I dreaded a break-up more than a relationship—and you…' He smiled at her. 'You just carried right on.'

'Not on the inside.'

She'd never admitted it to anyone, not just about Jed but about her fears and her thoughts and how more than anyone in the world she hated confrontation, hated rows, and that, yes, she had been running away. 'I've got to stop avoiding rows…'

'I think it's nice that you do.'

But Jasmine shook her head.

'You're a lot stronger than you think.'

She didn't feel very strong sometimes and she told him a little of how it felt to be related to two very strong women who were so accomplished in everything they did.

'Jasmine,' Jed asked. 'What do you want?'

'Meaning?'

'What do you want?'

She thought for a moment, about Simon safe and warm and sleeping in his cot and her job that she loved and her little home right on the beach and a relationship that looked like it might be working.

'What I've got,' Jasmine said.

'And you've worked for it,' Jed pointed out. 'You could have listened to your mum and sister and been some high-powered lawyer or doctor and hating every minute of it, or you could be working in the fracture clinic because the hours are better, but instead you've stood your ground and you do a job you love... And,' Jed added, 'despite a lousy relationship you've got an amazing son and your heart's back out there. I'd say you're pretty strong.'

And he was right. She had everything she wanted, even if wasn't what her mother or sister might choose. She did, even if it was misguided at times, follow her heart.

'I do want a little bit more,' Jasmine said.

'What?' He moved in for a kiss.

'White walls,' Jasmine whispered. 'I'm on my fourth coat.'

And he looked at walls that were still green tinged and he started to laugh. 'Did you put on an undercoat?'

He saw her frown.

'Jasmine,' he groaned. 'I'll do it at the weekend. But for now...'

It was bliss to be kissed by him again, bliss to be back in his arms and to know there were no secrets between them now, nothing more to know.

Except...

'How did your interview go?' She wriggled out of his kiss—there was so much she had missed out on.

'Don't worry about that now.'

'But how did it go?'

'Very well,' Jed said. 'I should know tomorrow.'

'How did Penny go?'

'Just leave it, huh? Suffice it to say I'm quietly confident but I'll be fine if it doesn't come off.'

'Sure?'

'Sure.'

And then he got back to kissing her and this time she didn't halt him with questions. This time it was just about them, at least until Simon woke up. This time she didn't hesitate, and brought him straight through.

'Jed!' Simon smiled when he saw him.

'You outed us to Penny!' Jed grinned and then he looked at Jasmine. 'We need to go out.'

'I know,' she said. 'I'll speak to Ruby. I can't just…'

'I didn't mean it like that,' Jed said. 'I mean that we need to announce ourselves to the world before Simon does.'

'I think he already has,' Jasmine said. 'Can't you feel them all watching us?'

He just grinned and then he said what he was thinking and it was far nicer than having to censor every word and thought, so much better than having to hold back. 'Do you want to come to the A and E ball?'

'It's too soon.'

'Not for me,' Jed said. 'Though I will probably only be able to stay till ten, so you might be deposited home early, but I want people to know about us. It isn't too soon for me.'

'I meant…' Jasmine laughed '…that it's too soon for me to organise anything. The ball's tomorrow—and I'm working till four and I haven't got anything to wear.'

'You'll look lovely whatever you wear.'

'That's the most stupid thing I've ever heard…' Did he have not a clue as to how much went into getting ready for this sort of thing? Everyone who was going had the afternoon off and had been talking about dresses and shoes for weeks.

'I'm not going to argue with you.' Jed smiled. 'After all, I know how much you hate it. So I'm just going to tell you instead that we're going to the ball tomorrow and I expect you to be ready when I get here.'

CHAPTER SEVENTEEN

A BIT MORE notice would have been nice.

Lisa and Penny were bright orange, thanks to their spray tans, which they would shower off before their hairdresser appointments, Jasmine thought darkly, or after they'd picked up their thousand-dollar dresses from the dry cleaner's.

They were working on a head injury—their newly extended and painted nails hidden under plastic gloves. Penny wanted him admitted to ICU, except there weren't any beds at Peninsula, though they had been told there *might* be one available later on in the afternoon.

'Nope.' Penny shook her head. 'He'll have to be transferred.'

'Okay,' Lisa said. 'Do you want me to do a ring around?' She looked at Jasmine. 'You go and have your break.' As Jasmine opened her mouth to argue, Lisa overrode her. 'You might have to transfer him,' she pointed out, 'so go and have a break now.'

Jasmine didn't have time for a break.

Instead, she raced up to CCU. She was incredibly nervous about tonight and terribly aware of the lack of anything suitable in her wardrobe and she was determined to dash to the shops at lunchtime. She knew it might be her only chance to visit her mum but as she swept in to see her, Jasmine halted when she saw Jed standing there beside her bed.

'Hi, there.' Jasmine smiled, but it was a wary one, because Jed wasn't her mother's doctor. He hadn't even been involved in her admission. 'Is everything okay?'

'Everything's fine.' Louise smiled, but Jasmine was still cautious.

'Your mum's temperature was up a bit up this morning,' Jed explained. 'And Penny's stuck in with that head injury and insisted that I check things out…' He rolled his eyes. 'She's got a slight chest infection but they're onto it with antibiotics and your mum's physio has been increased.' He gave Louise a smile. 'Now that I've seen for myself that you'll live and have spoken to your doctor, I'd better get back down there and reassure your elder daughter.'

She hardly waited till he was out of the door and had she looked over her shoulder she would have seen Jed shake his head as Jasmine anxiously picked up her mother's charts and saw that her temperature had indeed been rather high but was on its way down.

'Jasmine.' Her mum was stern. 'I've got a chest infection.'

'I know.'

'It's not a big deal,' her mum said, and saw Jasmine's anxious eyes. 'Okay, it could be, but they're straight onto it. They've taken loads of bloods and they've got me up and walking and coughing on the hour. It's my own stupid fault,' Louise admitted. 'It hurt to take a deep breath and to cough and I didn't really listen when they said to increase my painkillers. I thought I was doing better by having less.'

'Mum.' Jasmine let out a frustrated sigh. 'You're so...'

'Stubborn.'

'I could think of a few other words,' Jasmine said. 'Why wouldn't you take the medication?'

'I just wanted to go home and I thought the sooner I got off the strong stuff the sooner they'd release me.'

'And because of that you'll probably be stuck here for another couple of days.'

'Well, we don't always do what's right for us, do we?' Louise admitted. 'But I am learning.' And to prove it she pushed her pain medication button and the little pump whirred into life. 'See?'

'I spoke with the insurance and the travel agent,' Jasmine said, 'and you shall have your cruise, but not for a few months.' She saw her mum rest back on the pillow. 'I brought in some brochures—you get to choose all over again.'

'That's such a relief,' Louise said. 'That means that I can help you out a bit more.'

'Mum, the only person you need to be concentrating on right now is you. I'm getting in the swing of things now. Vanessa and I are going to work out our nights and our late shifts, and we've got Ruby. I just needed you for the first few weeks.'

'And I made it hard to ask,' Louise said. 'I'm sorry.'

'Don't be sorry.'

'I am.'

'You gave me a push,' Jasmine said. 'I knew what I was going to get when I decided to come home—and you have helped. I couldn't have started back on shifts without you. But...' Jasmine took a deep breath, '...I'm not going to apply to work in the fracture clinic, I'm going to stay in Emergency. It's what I'm good at. And it might be a juggle, but…'

'You'll sort it.'

'I will,' Jasmine said, feeling far more positive.

'I don't remember much of my time in there, but…' she took her daughter's hand, '…I do know what was done for me and I've seen the nurses hard at it on ICU and in here. I'm proud of what you do, Jasmine, and I'm sorry I haven't been more supportive. I get it now.'

'Good.'

'And it breaks my heart what Penny had to go through, and I am so glad you were spared from that, but apart from that, I can't think of anyone I'd rather have looking after me than you. Don't let your career go.'

'I'm not going to.'

'No matter how easy it is to drop down to part time or—'

'Mum! I've got a one-year-old to support so dropping my hours down isn't even on the agenda. Not for the next seventeen years at least.'

'He seems nice.' Louise's head jerked to the door. 'Jed.'

'He is.'

'Penny said that you two have been seeing each other.'

'Mum!' Jasmine was firm. 'It's early days. Neither of us wants to rush into anything and there's Simon to think of. Still—' she couldn't help but share the news, '—I'm going to the A and E ball with him tonight.'

'What are you wearing?'

'I don't know yet.' Jasmine ignored her mother's horrified expression. 'I'm going to look at lunchtime.'

'In the village?'

Jasmine closed her eyes. There were about two clothes

shops near enough to get to in her lunch break and, no, she didn't think they would have a massive selection of ballgowns to choose from.

'I'd lend you something, but…'

'I'm not borrowing something from my mum!'

'I've got very good taste,' Louise said, 'and a black dress is a black dress, but…' she ran an eye over Jasmine '…it wouldn't fit.'

'Just keep pushing that pain medication button, Mum.' Jasmine smiled. 'You might need it soon.'

'What about your wedding dress?'

'Please.'

'Well, it's not really a wedding dress, is it?' Louise pointed out. 'It would look lovely.'

'No.' Jasmine gave her mum a kiss. 'I have to get back.'

'Are you getting your hair done?'

'Yes!' Jasmine lied. 'Don't worry, I'm not going to let the side down.'

'I know. Can you drop by on your way?'

'Mum!' That was too cringy for words.

'Penny is.'

'Oh, Mum,' Jasmine said. 'I think I preferred the old you.'

'Tough.' Louise smiled. 'You've got a new mum now. Right, you have a lovely day and I'll look forward to seeing you this evening.'

Jasmine headed back down to Emergency and gave a brief nod to Penny, who was sitting at the nursing station writing up notes, and beside her was Jed.

'Have you seen Mum?'

Jasmine blinked in surprise. 'I've just been,' Jasmine said. 'She looks well.'

'What's her temp?'

'Down to thirty-seven point five.'

'Good.'

'Well, she's certainly changed her tune,' Jasmine said to Jed as Penny was called back into Resus. 'I'm actually being acknowledged.' She made sure no one was listening. 'Have you heard?'

'What?'

'Jed!' He was so annoying sometimes. 'About the job,' she mouthed.

'Not yet!' he mouthed back. And then she remembered something. 'This is too embarrassing for words, but on the way to the ball Mum wants me to pop in.'

'No problem.'

'For two minutes.'

'It's no big deal,' Jed assured her.

'For you maybe,' Jasmine grumbled. 'I think they bypassed the old mum when they did surgery.'

'Jasmine.' She heard a rather familiar call from Greg and, jumping off her seat, she dashed into Resus to see the head injury Penny had been working on looking significantly worse. His arms were extending to painful stimuli and Penny was sedating him and getting ready to intubate.

Penny was marvellous, barking out her orders as always, but she actually called for Jed's help when the anaesthetist didn't arrive. Whatever way you looked at it, she was fantastic at her job, just a cow around the staff. That was to say, all the staff, so she didn't deliberately take it personally when Penny told her none too politely to hurry up as Jasmine loaded a syringe with propofol, an oily drug that was a bit slow to draw up. And she really was confident in her work. Penny's hands weren't even shaking as she intubated the patient, Jasmine noticed.

And then Lisa spoke and as Jasmine pulled up some more medication she noticed that her own hands were shaking.

'There's an ICU bed at Melbourne Central. The chopper is already out so I've called for MICA and a police escort.' She told the anaesthetist the same when he arrived and then she told Jasmine to prepare the patient and get herself ready.

'It will be fine,' Jed said just a little while later when Mark and his colleague arrived and transferred the patient to the stretcher. 'Jasmine, it will be.'

'I know.'

'No one's going to say anything.'

'And if they do?'

'They won't,' Jed said. 'But if they do, just tell them to mind their own business.'

He gave her shoulder a squeeze. 'If I don't see you before, I'll pick you up about six-thirty.'

Oh, God… Jasmine would have closed her eyes, except she had to move now, had to follow the stretcher into the ambulance. No, she wasn't going to be buying a dress this lunchtime, neither would she be sorting out her hair.

Instead she was going back to Melbourne Central.

With a police escort they practically flew down the freeway. The patient was stable throughout and Craig, the anaesthetist, was very calm, as were the paramedics. It was Jasmine whose heart was hammering as they approached the hospital she had loved and the place it had hurt so much to leave.

'Are you okay, Jasmine?' Mark asked, before they climbed out.

'Sure.'

'No one's going to eat you.'

'I know.'

Of course, it was a bit of an anticlimax. The hospital didn't suddenly stop just because she was back. In fact, she didn't recognise any of the staff on ICU as she handed the patient over.

The paramedics were going to be taking Jasmine and Craig back to Peninsula, but Mark wanted to take a break before the return journey.

'We'll just grab some lunch at the canteen,' Mark told her.

'I'll meet you back at the ambulance,' Jasmine told him. Tempting as it was to hide out in the canteen, Jasmine decided that she was tired of running away from things, tired of feeling guilty over mistakes that weren't even hers, so feeling nervous but brave she walked into Emergency.

'Hi.' She smiled at a face she didn't recognise. 'I was wondering—'

'Jasmine!' She never got to finish her sentence as Hannah, the charge nurse, came rushing over. 'Where have you been?'

'I moved back home.'

'You never even let us know you'd had your baby. Martha said that she heard it was a boy.'

And she was back and her friends were crowding around her, looking at pictures of Simon on her phone. Hearing their enthusiasm, she realised just how badly she had misjudged her friendships and she started crying.

'He was a bastard,' Hannah said when Jasmine told her why. 'Of course nobody thought you were involved.'

'Everybody was so weird around me.'

'We were embarrassed,' Martha said. 'Upset for you.' She gave Jasmine a hug. 'You're better off without him, you know.'

'Oh, God, do I know.'

'Does that mean you're coming back?' Hannah asked.

She thought for a moment, because she could come back and part of her wanted to come back except, Jasmine realised then, just as she had told Jed, she was very happy with what she had now.

'Maybe one day.' Jasmine smiled and then of course they asked if she was seeing anyone and she was through with covering things up and so she said yes.

'His name's Jed,' Jasmine said. 'Jed Devlin.'

'I know that name.' Hannah frowned. 'Where do I know that name from?'

'He came for an interview here,' Jasmine said.

'That's right.' Hannah nodded and then waved in direction of the door. 'I think your transport's ready.' Jasmine turned and there were the paramedics. 'Don't be a stranger,' Hannah warned. Then she laughed. 'Well, I guess you won't be now.'

Jasmine had no idea what Hannah meant, but she was on too much of a high to think about it, and then when she realised she still had nothing to wear tonight and she wasn't going to get to the shops, she was far too panicked to dwell on Hannah's words, especially when they hit traffic on the way home.

'Can't you put on the sirens?' Jasmine grumbled, but the paramedics just laughed. 'Some of us are going out tonight.'

CHAPTER EIGHTEEN

THANK GOD FOR heated rollers and quick-dry nail varnish, Jasmine thought as somehow she cobbled herself together, cringing as she pulled her old wedding dress on.

It didn't look remotely like a wedding dress.

It was a dark blue silk that her mother had said matched her eyes, and the strange thing was, as she looked in the mirror, she looked better in it than she had on the big day.

Then she had been sixteen weeks pregnant and bloated and miserable and not particularly sure that she wasn't making the biggest mistake of her life, and, no, she hadn't been particularly excited at the prospect of her wedding night.

Now she had curves and a smile and couldn't wait for the formalities to be over just to get Jed into bed!

'Wow,' Ruby said when she opened the door. 'You look gorgeous. I love the dress.'

'Thanks.' Jasmine smiled.

'Where did you get it?'

'I've had it for ages.' Jasmine blushed and mumbled something about a boutique in the city as she stuffed her bag with lipstick and keys. 'I don't think I'll be late back,' she told Ruby. 'Jed has to go into work and cover for Penny.'

'All you have to worry about is enjoying yourself,' Ruby said. 'He'll be fine.'

She knew that Simon would be fine.

It was two other people she was more worried about tonight.

Surely they wouldn't tell them about the job today, Jasmine reasoned. It was the A and E ball tonight so they would no doubt wait till next week to give the verdict.

Oh, God, Jasmine thought, putting in her earrings, she was torn.

Family first, she told herself, except she knew about the delays that had been caused in Jed's career. He was older than Penny and he wasn't where he thought he should be in his career.

And here he was at her door.

Her heart was hammering for different reasons when she first saw him in a tux.

'Wow.' Jed gave a whistle of appreciation. 'I told you you'd look lovely.'

'Wow to you too,' Jasmine said.

'I thought you said you had nothing to wear. Jasmine, you didn't go spending a fortune, did you?'

'No, no,' Jasmine said. 'I've had this for ages. I didn't know if it would fit!' Quickly she tried to change the subject. 'Have you heard about the job?'

'We'll talk about it later.' He sort of nodded his head in the direction of Ruby. 'We ought to go, especially if you want to drop in to see your mum.'

'I feel stupid walking through the hospital dressed like this.'

'It will be nice for her,' Jed said. 'And knowing that place, Penny will get called just as she gets into her dress and have to do something urgent and be swanning around Resus in pink satin.'

'I guess,' Jasmine said. 'Though I can't see her in pink satin.' Jed smiled, but she could tell he was a little on edge. Maybe he was having second thoughts about them being seen out together so soon and she told him so.

'You're being daft.'

It was worth going in just to see the smile on her mum's face.

'You look great.' Louise smiled. 'You both do.'

'I'm just going to go and ring the unit and check it's okay,' Jed said, and she knew it was because staff were a bit thin on the ground, but it also gave her a chance for a little bit longer with her mum.

'You look so much better.'

'I feel it,' Louise said. 'I told you your wedding dress would be perfect!'

'Shhh!' Jasmine warned. 'I don't want him knowing.'

'Now.' Louise was back to practical. 'Your sister's got something to tell you, some big news.' And her heart should have surged for Penny, except first it sank for Jed and then it surged back up because she was truly torn. 'It's big news and even if it's a bit hard to hear it, I think it's really important that you be pleased for her.'

'Of course I'll be pleased.'

'I know,' Louise said. 'I can't say anything, I don't want to spoil things for her, and I guess that it's her news to share, but just keep that smile fixed on.'

'I will.'

She gave her mum a kiss and then walked out to where Jed was just hanging up the phone.

'Let's get going.'

He was quiet on the car ride there and if he was just

a touch tense, at least Jasmine knew why, but he took her hand and they walked in together and she knew that if he was being a bit quiet it had nothing to do with her.

'Hi, there!' Penny came over all smiles, and kissed Jed's cheek and then Jasmine's too.

'You look amazing,' Jasmine said, because Penny did. There was a glow in her cheeks and a smile that was just a little bit smug, and she didn't blame Jed when he excused himself to have a word with Mr Dean.

'Why are you wearing your wedding dress?' Penny asked the second he was out of earshot.

'Because I had about ten minutes' warning about tonight,' Jasmine said. 'And don't tell anyone.'

'Isn't that a bit twisted?' Penny wrinkled her nose. 'Doesn't that make you a bit of a saddo?'

'Stop it!' Jasmine said, but she started to laugh. Penny was such a cow at times, but she was also very funny.

'Any news?' Jasmine asked.

'Not here, Jasmine,' Penny warned.

'Oh, stop it,' Jasmine said. 'No one can read my lips. You got the job, didn't you? I know you did.' She looked at her sister. 'I thought we were going to be more honest from now on.'

'Jasmine,' Penny warned.

'Well, I'm thrilled for you.' She really was. 'Honestly.'

'Jasmine, will you please shut up?' Penny gave a sigh of irritation then beckoned her towards the ladies. Of course it was crowded, so they went outside and Penny waited till they were about twenty metres from anyone before she spoke,

'I did get offered the job,' Penny said, 'and before you jump up and down on the spot and get all emotional and then start worrying about Jed…'

Jasmine took a deep breath.

'I withdrew my application.'

Jasmine literally felt her jaw drop. 'Why would you do that?'

'Because,' Jasmine said, 'and I never thought I'd hear myself say this, but some things are more important in life.'

'Your career is…' Jasmine buttoned her lip but Penny just laughed.

'Exactly,' she said. 'There needs to be more. I've been a terrible aunt,' Penny said, 'and an appalling sister, because I've been so incredibly jealous of you. I always have been. And I guess I still am. I want what you have.' And she smiled as Jasmine frowned. 'Not Jed, you idiot. The other guy in your life.'

'A baby?'

'It seems Mr Dean was right. They train you up and what do you go and do…?'

'You're pregnant?'

'Not yet,' Penny said. 'But I'm hoping to be in the not-too-distant future, and from everything I've heard about IVF, well, I'm not going to be the sunniest person.'

'Penny!' Jasmine was stunned.

'I'm in my mid-thirties and I just…' Penny gave a tight shrug. 'At the moment I have about sixty-three minutes a week to devote to a relationship. There are not many men who would put up with that.'

'There might be.'

'Well, I want my baby,' Penny said. 'And I've thought long and hard and I'll work right up to the last minute and then—'

'But IVF?' Jasmine queried. 'Don't you just need a donor?'

'I tried for a baby with Vince.' Jasmine watched her sister's eyes, which were always so sharp, actually fill with tears. 'We had a few problems.' She looked at her sister. 'Or rather I had a few problems in that department. It meant IVF and Vince and I…' She swallowed her tears down. 'Well, I think we weren't really up to the challenge.'

'Is that why you broke up?'

'In part.'

'Why couldn't you talk to me?'

'I am now,' Penny said, and Jasmine realised what her mum had meant about some big news. But, no, she didn't need to be told to keep her smile on, she was genuinely thrilled for her sister. 'You have to give me my injections, though.'

'I can't wait to stick another needle in you.' Jasmine grinned and gave Penny a hug.

'And I'm not giving up my career,' Penny said. 'I'm just not complicating things for now. I have no idea how I'm going to work things out.'

'You will,' Jasmine said.

'I think I'll have to get a nanny.'

'We can share one.' Jasmine grinned.

'I want this,' Penny said. 'And I'm not waiting around for Mr Right. Anyway, I've seen both you and mum stuff up—we have terrible taste in men.'

'I guess.'

'Not this time, though.' Penny smiled. 'Mind you, don't you go telling him I got offered the job.'

'Penny! I'm sick of lying.'

'I mean it. If he has got the job and that's what he's all worked up about, the last thing he needs is to be told

I turned it down. Just be all happy and celebrate when he gets the news.'

'Do you think he's got it?' Jasmine wasn't so sure—Jed seemed really tense.

'I'm pretty sure. There was an external applicant who was pretty impressive but I think Mr Dean wants to keep it in-house. He should hear any time soon.'

She had a terrible feeling that he already had.

Jed was lovely as they drove back from the ball a couple of hours later, but she could tell that he had something on his mind—it had stung when she had thought he had lost the job to Penny. She knew how his career had been sidetracked dealing with what he had, but losing it to an outsider would really hurt.

'Where are we going?'

Only then had she noticed they were driving to the city.

'Somewhere nice.'

'But you have to work.'

'Nope.' He grinned. 'Mr Dean arranged a locum, well, not really a locum—he's going to be working there in a few weeks so it's good if he gets a feel for the place.'

She looked over and tried to read his expression.

'Working there?'

'The new consultant.' He gave a small grimace.

'Oh, Jed.' She really didn't know what to say. 'I know it's hard for you…'

'Hard on me?' He turned and looked at Jasmine. 'It's hard on you, though Penny didn't look as upset as I thought she'd be,' Jed admitted. 'I thought she'd be savage.' He shook his head. 'She seemed fine.'

Jasmine looked out of the window to the bay. Penny had been right. Working in the same department was way too complicated. She could hardly tell Jed the real reason Penny was so delighted and she definitely didn't want to tell him that Penny had actually turned down the job.

They chatted about this and that but she could feel his tension and she was so irritated that they had told the applicants today of all days. Couldn't they just have enjoyed tonight?

'We can't stay out too long.' Jasmine glanced at her watch—half an hour really, if she was going to be back by midnight, though maybe she could stretch it till half past. It was hardly his fault. He just wanted to go out somewhere nice and wasn't used to factoring in a one-year-old and his babysitter.

'What are we doing here?' she asked as they pulled up at a very nice hotel.

'I told you I wanted to take you somewhere nice.'

'Just a drink at the bar, then.' She hoped he hadn't booked for dinner. He popped the boot and as Jasmine stepped out of the car, she frowned as he gave his name to park it and frowned even more at the sight of her rather tatty case being hauled out.

'Jed?'

'Ruby packed it,' Jed said. 'It's all sorted.'

'Oh.'

They went to check in. It was the nicest thing he could have done for her, but she felt terrible because surely he had been planning a celebration, or maybe he hadn't factored in that he'd know.

It was like holiday where it was raining and everyone was pretending it didn't matter, all grimly determined to enjoy themselves, and she would…she was. Jasmine was thrilled to have a night away with him, she just knew how hard this must be for him.

'Wow!' She stepped into the hotel room and tried not to notice the champagne and two glasses. Instead, she stared out at the view but Jed poured two glasses and it tasted fantastic and, yes, it was fantastic to be together.

'I am sorry about the job,' Jasmine said.

'Shhh,' he said. 'Let's just celebrate.'

'Cheers!'

'You don't know what we're celebrating,' Jed said.

'That we're here's good enough for me.'

'And me,' Jed said, and then he smiled. '"Oh, ye of little faith".'

She didn't understand. 'Sorry?'

He pulled back one of the curtains. 'Have a look over there. What do you see?' It was just a busy city. 'Over there.' He pointed to a tall building. 'That's where I'm going to be working. I got offered a consultant's position on Thursday, so I withdrew my application.'

'Oh!' She could have thumped him. 'You let me drive all that way thinking you were disappointed!'

'No,' Jed said. 'I knew that you *were* disappointed—it's awful for Penny. I really thought when I took the position at Melbourne Central that Penny was a certainty for the job. I think Mr Dean's really got it wrong. The new guy seems great by all accounts, but it's going to be tough on your sister.'

'No, you don't understand.' She opened her mouth, but again she couldn't say anything.

'What?'

Jasmine shook her head. 'Leave it.'

'I can't.'

'You can.'

'I can't.'

Jasmine was firm. 'She's my sister.'

She looked over to where he'd be working. 'I thought you were happy at Peninsula.'

'I've been incredibly happy,' Jed said. 'I applied to a few hospitals when I first thought of moving here and it was a close-run thing. I love big city hospitals but when Mr Dean hinted at a consultancy… Anyway, Central rang me last week and asked if I'd be interested in a more senior position than the one I interviewed for last year, and given the tension at work, given a lot of things, the choice was actually easy.'

'That's good,' Jasmine said, trying to mask the little edge of disappointment in her voice, that just when they were finding each other he was upping sticks, but, still, it was just an hour or so away.

'I like to keep work and home separate,' Jed said.

'I know that.'

'And I haven't been doing a very good job of it of late.'

He started to kiss her and then pulled his head back. 'You're sulking.'

'No.' She looked up at him and she was too scared to admit it, because he meant so much more than she dared reveal. They'd agreed they were going to take things slowly and, yes, they were back on track, but maybe once he got to a big hospital, maybe when things were more difficult, when Simon was sick and he was on call and it all became too hard to have a single mum as a girl-friend who lived a good hour away, maybe then things would go wrong for them.

'It's been a hell of a week.'

'And now it's over,' Jed said. 'Now you can enjoy being spoiled.' He gave her a smile. 'Come on, tell me, how come Penny's looking so pleased if she didn't get the job.'

Jasmine closed her eyes. 'Actually, come to think of it, it's a good job that you're going to Melbourne Central. I'm not breaking my sister's confidence.' She looked at him.

'Fair enough.'

'She's family.'

'I'm not arguing.' Jed grinned. 'I think you want to, though.'

'I don't.'

Jasmine didn't. She didn't want anything to spoil this night. 'So...' She forced her voice to be upbeat. 'When do you start?'

'Four weeks,' Jed said. 'It's going to be fantastic— it's a great hospital.'

'Good.'

'It's everything I want.'

He pulled her into his arms and he was smiling. She would not ruin this night, would not nit-pick, but how come he was so happy to be leaving? How come he had been so tense all night? Though he wasn't tense now, he was *delighted* with his good news, thrilled to be moving an hour away, and she swallowed down her tears.

'I can't wait to start,' Jed said. 'And tomorrow I thought I might go and look for somewhere to live.'

Some bachelor city apartment, Jasmine thought bitterly, but she kept her smile there.

'The staff there seem really friendly,' he added.

She thought of Hannah, who was gorgeous and flirted like crazy, and Martha, and the wild parties they often had, and he would be there and she would be home with Simon.

'And I can't wait…'

'Okay.' Her lips were taut with smiling. 'I'm thrilled for you.'

She reached for her glass as she did not want to argue; she took a sip of champagne and swallowed down a row, but it was fizzing. Yes, she was happy for him, yes, she was thrilled, but… 'Do you have to keep rubbing it in?'

She didn't get why he was smiling.

'Sorry?'

'Do you have to keep telling me how *thrilled* you are to be leaving, how fantastic it is to be moving away?'

'Come on, Jasmine.' He grinned. 'Don't spoil tonight with a row.'

'I want one!' She did. For the first time in her life she wanted her row and stuff it if it was an expensive one. So what if she was spoiling a wonderful night? Did he have to be quite so insensitive?

'Go for it.'

'I will,' Jasmine said. 'I'm thrilled for you. I really am, but do you have to keep going on about it?' She just said it. 'Do you have to keep telling me how delighted you are to be going away and all the parties…'

'I never said anything about parties.'

'Oh, but there will be.'

And he just grinned.

'And I'll be home with Simon and you'll be an hour away and, yes, I am happy for you and, no, I didn't expect you to take Simon and me into consideration, but I can't keep grinning like an idiot when the fact is you're moving away.' She started to cry. 'And I don't understand why you're laughing.'

'Because I love how you row.'

And he pulled her into him. 'I've been goading you.'

'Why?'

'Because.'

'Because what?'

'I want just a smidge of obsession.'

'Well, you've got it.' And he kissed her and it was lovely. She'd said what she thought, had had a good row and no one was any the worse for it. Then he stopped kissing her and looked at her for a very long time.

'I am pleased for you. I honestly am. I know you'll love it there.' And she realised then what Hannah had meant when she'd said that she'd see her around. If she was going out with Jed she'd be with him at times. 'I'm just sad you're leaving, that's all.'

'I have to,' Jed said. 'Because I'm not working alongside a woman who turned down my proposal.' And he took out a box containing a ring but she didn't even look at it properly, just looked straight back at him. 'And if she doesn't turn it down then I'm working in the same department as my wife and sister-in-law. That would be way too complicated and I already have trouble enough concentrating on work when you're around. So which one is it?'

'The complicated one,' Jasmine said, and watched as he put a ring on her finger.

'It won't be complicated for long,' he assured her. 'I'm taking time off before I start my new job and for the next few weeks I'm going to take some time to get to know that son of yours and you're going to get to know me properly. We'll go to Sydney and meet my family. We'll just take some time. I don't want you to feel you're being rushed into anything again. We'll wait as long as it takes for you to feel okay with it.'

'I already am.' She had never been more sure of anything in her life. 'And I don't feel as if I'm rushing into things this time. I know.'

'I know too,' Jed said. 'And you're coming to look for somewhere to live with me. Midway, maybe? Or we can just carry on as we are and I'll sort out the travel, but I promise you that you and Simon will always be my first consideration.'

She believed him, she really did, and her heart filled not just for her own happiness but because her son was going to have such an amazing man to help raise him, for all the happy times to come.

'Mum's going to have another heart attack when she finds out.'

'She already knows,' Jed said. 'What, do you think I'd ask you to marry me without asking for her permission?'

'You asked her?' So that was what her mum had been banging on about not dropping her hours or losing her career—she already knew.

'Of course I asked her.'

'You're an old-fashioned thing, aren't you?'

'Yep,' Jed said. 'But I'm filthy-minded too. I want to do you in your wedding dress.'

She blinked.

'I'm sure you will.'

'I mean this one.'

She just about died of embarrassment, right there on the spot. 'You knew?'

'Your mum told me.' He smiled, and then pulled her back into his arms. 'And now, seeing as I'm almost family, you can tell me what's going on with Penny.' She started to, but he stopped her.

'Not yet.' He was kissing her face, kissing her mouth, and making her feel wanted and beautiful in her wedding dress for the very first time, as he told her just how much the future was theirs. 'We've got ages.'

* * * * *

Mills & Boon® Hardback

July 2013

ROMANCE

His Most Exquisite Conquest	Emma Darcy
One Night Heir	Lucy Monroe
His Brand of Passion	Kate Hewitt
The Return of Her Past	Lindsay Armstrong
The Couple who Fooled the World	Maisey Yates
Proof of Their Sin	Dani Collins
In Petrakis's Power	Maggie Cox
A Shadow of Guilt	Abby Green
Once is Never Enough	Mira Lyn Kelly
The Unexpected Wedding Guest	Aimee Carson
A Cowboy To Come Home To	Donna Alward
How to Melt a Frozen Heart	Cara Colter
The Cattleman's Ready-Made Family	Michelle Douglas
Rancher to the Rescue	Jennifer Faye
What the Paparazzi Didn't See	Nicola Marsh
My Boyfriend and Other Enemies	Nikki Logan
The Gift of a Child	Sue MacKay
How to Resist a Heartbreaker	Louisa George

MEDICAL

Dr Dark and Far-Too Delicious	Carol Marinelli
Secrets of a Career Girl	Carol Marinelli
A Date with the Ice Princess	Kate Hardy
The Rebel Who Loved Her	Jennifer Taylor

Mills & Boon® Large Print
July 2013

ROMANCE

Playing the Dutiful Wife	Carol Marinelli
The Fallen Greek Bride	Jane Porter
A Scandal, a Secret, a Baby	Sharon Kendrick
The Notorious Gabriel Diaz	Cathy Williams
A Reputation For Revenge	Jennie Lucas
Captive in the Spotlight	Annie West
Taming the Last Acosta	Susan Stephens
Guardian to the Heiress	Margaret Way
Little Cowgirl on His Doorstep	Donna Alward
Mission: Soldier to Daddy	Soraya Lane
Winning Back His Wife	Melissa McClone

HISTORICAL

The Accidental Prince	Michelle Willingham
The Rake to Ruin Her	Julia Justiss
The Outrageous Belle Marchmain	Lucy Ashford
Taken by the Border Rebel	Blythe Gifford
Unmasking Miss Lacey	Isabelle Goddard

MEDICAL

The Surgeon's Doorstep Baby	Marion Lennox
Dare She Dream of Forever?	Lucy Clark
Craving Her Soldier's Touch	Wendy S. Marcus
Secrets of a Shy Socialite	Wendy S. Marcus
Breaking the Playboy's Rules	Emily Forbes
Hot-Shot Doc Comes to Town	Susan Carlisle

Mills & Boon® Hardback
August 2013

ROMANCE

The Billionaire's Trophy	Lynne Graham
Prince of Secrets	Lucy Monroe
A Royal Without Rules	Caitlin Crews
A Deal with Di Capua	Cathy Williams
Imprisoned by a Vow	Annie West
Duty At What Cost?	Michelle Conder
The Rings that Bind	Michelle Smart
An Inheritance of Shame	Kate Hewitt
Faking It to Making It	Ally Blake
Girl Least Likely to Marry	Amy Andrews
The Cowboy She Couldn't Forget	Patricia Thayer
A Marriage Made in Italy	Rebecca Winters
Miracle in Bellaroo Creek	Barbara Hannay
The Courage To Say Yes	Barbara Wallace
All Bets Are On	Charlotte Phillips
Last-Minute Bridesmaid	Nina Harrington
Daring to Date Dr Celebrity	Emily Forbes
Resisting the New Doc In Town	Lucy Clark

MEDICAL

Miracle on Kaimotu Island	Marion Lennox
Always the Hero	Alison Roberts
The Maverick Doctor and Miss Prim	Scarlet Wilson
About That Night...	Scarlet Wilson

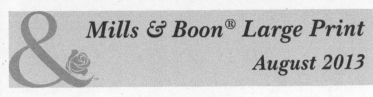

Mills & Boon® Large Print
August 2013

ROMANCE

HISTORICAL

MEDICAL